LO!
JACARANDA

*A Spanish Gypsy's Cante Jondo
(deep song of the caves)*

WRITTEN AND ILLUSTRATED BY HARRY FREIERMUTH

Order this book online at www.trafford.com
or email orders@trafford.com

Most Trafford titles are also available at major online book retailers.

Print information available on the last page.

ISBN: 978-1-4907-5344-7 (sc)
      978-1-4907-5345-4 (e)

Library of Congress Control Number: 2014922899

Trafford rev. 01/08/2015

 www.trafford.com

North America & international
toll-free: 1 888 232 4444 (USA & Canada)
fax: 812 355 4082

This book is dedicated to Blessed Ceferino Giménez Malla, "El Pele," the patron of the Romani people, and to Romani (Gypsy) families worldwide.

CHAPTER 1

Sunshine hid the pains of joy,

Illegitimate.

Moonlight beamed the joy of pain,

Legitimate love.

—Siguiriya

A nd lo, twice was I born. My first birth was illegitimate. My second birth was legitimate. But I died.

It all happened in the countryside north of Cádiz, Spain, on May 15, 1750, at my legitimate father's Rancho del Hidalgo Francisco Moreno Gonzales.

My illegitimate mother, Safira the Gypsy, began suffering her birth pains on May 14, early in the morning, about cockcrow. She twisted and turned on her bed of straw in the dark shadows of the cave where she lived on the ranchero. Her breathing alternated between loud and faint as the pains of new life grew stronger and stronger. And lo, she yelled as loud as she could. No one heard or cared, or so it seemed. All the other Gypsies had gone off to work long before cockcrow.

Later that morning, Manuel Lopez, my father's overseer, heard a woman's cries. He looked into her cave and saw her struggling on her bed of straw. He held a cup of water to her cracked lips. Her eyes sparkled with a thank-you. He put the water jug within her reach and left. He thought, *Just another Gypsy givin' birth to another unfortunate Gypsy child.* With a quick smile, he wondered, *Who might be the father?*

My legitimate mother, Senora Margarita Moreno Gonzales, wife of Hidalgo Francisco Moreno Gonzales, began to feel her birth pains later in the morning. She had just finished her breakfast in her luxurious bedroom with its high open windows to let in the soft sunlight and the cool morning breeze from the Bay of Cádiz. She rested on her soft mattress covered by soft pastel-green silk sheets. Cashmere blankets, the color and fragrance of spring daffodils, kept her comfortable.

Her pains began like small drops of rain before a winter storm. Her maid moistened a small linen napkin in rose water to moisten her lady's brow, cheeks, and neck.

As the pains became more frequent and hurtful—like dark-purple grapes being crushed for wine—the maid placed a piece of leather strap the width of her lady's hand, as thick as her thumb, and moistened mint water into her lady's mouth. Her lady would bite on this to ease the pain and forestall unladylike screams.

In his own room, my father sat in his big leather chair. He enjoyed an early brandy and cigar. The maid kept him informed about his wife's condition. Each time she reported, he smiled and thanked her. Then he poured another brandy.

When Manuel Lopez made his midmorning report to my father, he mentioned his having heard a Gypsy in labor pains down at the caves.

My father asked, "Which Gypsy?"

"It could be Safira," he replied. "Her face was a mess. I gave her some water and left."

"Was anyone there to help?"

"No."

"Thank you, Manuel. I'll send someone to check on her."

"Yes, senor. I must go to check the cows in the north pasture."

"*Si*, Manuel. Do that and let me know how many new calves we have and can expect."

As soon as Manuel left, my father put on his sombrero and wandered down to the caves.

On entering Safira's cave, he heard her scream. Quick as a goat jumping a stream, he filled a pail full of water and found a rag to wet and cool her brow.

"That's better, that's better. Nothing's too good for my Safira."

"About time. About time someone came to help me."

"I just learned," he said. "Came as fast as I could."

"Don't put that water in my eyes," she said, grabbing his hand, "just my forehead."

"I'll try to help. But I'm not used to this."

"Too bad you didn't think about this when you were having so much fun a few months ago."

"I'll go get some of the grannies to help. They'll know what to do."

She screamed. She pulled his hand to her chest. "Feel that. That's my heart leapin' like a stag in heat."

She screamed again and again.

"I'll get two grannies," he stammered and fled from her cave.

In an open space in front of the caves, my father saw three old Gypsies stirring the fire under a large pot of boiling water.

"Can you fine ladies please look after Safira? She's going to have her baby and needs help."

"We're heatin' up the water for her now!" said the oldest-looking woman. "We know what to do, by cracky!" Then she spit on the fire to speed it up.

"But," said the granny with a patch over her right eye, "she ain't due for a while . . . maybe tonight, late . . . or tomorrow . . . early."

"Screams help," chimed in the third granny with three warts on the tip of her nose. "I know from experience." She gave him a knowing, toothless smile.

"Thank you," whispered my father. "I can't stand to hear her screams. I'll be back at the hacienda if you need my help."

Then he walked away, like a goat with a thistle up his ass.

Returning to his brandy and cigars, he waited.

The next day, after the cock crowed, the old granny with the patch over her right eye entered the kitchen door and asked, "Is the senor here? I must speak to him."

"Just a minute," replied the maid who answered the door. Then she relayed the granny's request to the cook, who told it to the headmistress, who went and knocked on the senor's door.

"Come in," the senor ordered.

"There's an old Gypsy who wants to talk with you."

"I'll be right down."

After putting on his sombrero, he walked to the kitchen door.

Recognizing the granny, my father beckoned her to go outside. They stopped by an old pine tree, out of earshot from the kitchen help staring out of the window.

"What's happened?" he whispered.

"The child's ready to pop any minute," gummed the nanny. "She don't scream no more. Just pants and wheezes lots o' hot air. An' grabs anything or person to stifle the pain."

"Let's go!" my father whispered. He grabbed her hand and dragged her to the cave.

My father pulled aside the long leafy vines that hung down to screen the entrance to Safira's cave. He looked in to see the other grannies ministering to Safira. Her bent knees were raised high above her undulating body, like a wild river crashing over boulders before descending over a waterfall. Then he saw me. The granny with three warts on her nose held me up high by my ankles. She gave my backside a quick slap. *Whaaa! Whaaa! Whaaa!* I cried. All smiled. The grannies bathed me and wrapped me in swaddling clothes. My mother received me with loving eyes and arms. She kissed me once on each eye. Then she kissed me once on my tiny lips. I felt her warmth and love.

My father woke from his stupor. He fumbled his way to the bed of straw. He knelt. He kissed my mother's forehead. Then he kissed mine too, like a bewildered butterfly buzzing his first buttercup.

In silence, we treasured this moment. Then my father rose to his feet. He sailed through the vines. He walked on sunlit air to his hacienda.

As my father neared his kitchen door, the head mistress cried out, "Oh, senor, come quick! The senora is in great pain."

"Take me to her at once."

"Yes, senor." Then she led him to her lady's bedroom.

My father entered his wife's room. He felt sorry for her suffering.

They had never loved each other. Theirs had been an arranged marriage. She had done her duty. She had borne him a son, Christabo, eight years ago. Now this would be their second child, if it lived. Their last two children had died at birth. The midwife and her assistants were doing their best. The warm towels were all in the right places to ease her pain. But something was not right. It was a feeling, an intuition that no one wanted to believe.

My father watched as his wife's breathing went from short gasps to a deep, long rattle, like a clock ticking out of time, then like the loud bongs of a grandfather's clock that kept bonging until everyone wanted to scream. But they couldn't.

Then they saw the new child, a girl. Dead.

My father picked up the stillborn. He tried to breathe life into her. But no life came.

The women cried and patted the senora's hands. She showed no response.

She too was dead.

The women looked at my father.

His face was covered with grief. Then a sudden idea flashed in his brain. He smiled. He laughed in secret. His hands held the child high in the air. He spoke, "I'll pray to Our Lady of the Lake. We have a shrine dedicated to her in our chapel. I'll pray that she will give life back to our little girl."

The women looked at him in amazement. Their mouths dropped wide open. Some thought, *He has gone mad.* Others surmised, *The strain of losing his wife and child has driven him insane.* They were in awe as my father grabbed the child and ran out the door and into the chapel next to the hacienda.

Inside the chapel, my father placed the body on the altar in front of Our Lady's statue. He knelt. He prayed, "Our Lady, please restore the life to my child. I know that you can do this. Please ask your Son, Jesus, to do this for me."

My father prayed these words. But in the back of his mind, he had another plan. He arose and rang the chapel bells. He pulled the rope like a wild man. He pulled so hard and fast that the bells clanged and clanged like a bevy of wild geese squawking their heads off for some unimaginable joy.

The peons and Gypsies gathered in front of the chapel. The question on their faces asked, *Why all this clatter?*

My father, with arms opened wide, spoke, "Please kneel here in this beautiful rose garden. Please pray to Our Lady to give life back to my dead daughter. I will pray inside the chapel. And I will call you to come in as soon as the miracle happens. Please pray as loud as you can. Keep your eyes shut, as tight as clamshells, so that nothing can distract your attention." Then he walked into the chapel, shut the door, and locked it.

At once, my father took the dead child, ran out the back door, and fled to Safira's cave.

In Safira's cave, my father knelt before Safira and their child. In a few words, he told about the death of his wife and her child.

Then with his violet-blue eyes of love, he looked into her deep black-brown eyes and sighed, "Safira, you are my one true love. I know we can never marry. But our daughter can be raised as my own legitimate daughter, in my hacienda. You can be her governess. You can live with her and care for her in my grand hacienda. You can leave this cave forever."

"But I will always be a Gypsy."

"Yes. You can sing your Gypsy lullabies and tell your Gypsy folktales to our daughter."

"But she will have your good name and be raised a true Spaniard."

"Yes. I will see to it that she has the best clothing and the finest schooling."

"But how can this be?" Safira smiled.

"Give your live child to me and take my dead child as your own. We'll say that your child died of fever. I'll bring our live child and place her on the altar before the statue of Our Lady of the Lake and proclaim a miracle. Only you and I and the Gypsies will know the truth. And we will all keep our secret, or else."

"Yes," Safira agreed.

"Thank you. I will send for you this evening. You will have new governess clothing and sleep in your own room with silk sheets and warm blankets."

My father unwrapped the dead child from her cashmere robe. My mother unwrapped me from my swaddling clothes. They switched babies. I was wrapped in the cashmere robe.

The dead baby was wrapped in my old swaddling clothes.

"Give me an hour. Then scream. The grannies will come. You can tell them our secret."

"OK. I'll trust you, senor." She smiled, thinking, *I know that I can trust Saint Sarah.*

My father nodded his thank-you. He smiled. With me in his arms, he ran to the chapel.

Once inside the chapel, my father placed me on the altar before the statue of Our Lady. Then he rang the bells. The bells rejoiced like a choir of angels singing and tossing fragrant rose petals.

My father opened the chapel's front door. With wide-open arms, he cried, "A miracle! Our Lady has given us a miracle. My child is alive."

The peons and Gypsies stopped their loud prayers and opened their eyes. They arose from their knees and shouted for joy. Flooding into the chapel, they stood awestruck in front of me.

I raised my hands and feet out of my cashmere robe and smiled at Our Lady. She smiled.

She knew the truth.

Padre Arturo and my father arranged for the proper time of mourning and the funeral Mass for the senora.

Safira and the Gypsies arranged to bury the dead child.

After the proper time of mourning had passed, Padre Arturo and my father made plans for my baptismal ceremony on the third Sunday in June 1750.

My father's hacienda sparkled like sunshine, knowing that this was my baptismal day.

The pork and the beef had been sacrificed. Manuel Lopez had seen to that. He had it hung to age in the shade of five oak trees. Gypsy boys waved palm fronds to scare away the insects.

Deep pits were dug. The meat was placed on a thick layer of wet fig and grape leaves. Another thick layer of wet leaves covered the meat. Then a thin layer of clean earth covered the leaves.

On top of that, a thick double layer of red-hot coals was placed. Another thick double layer of clean earth sealed it all off. It had simmered all night. Now it was ready.

The white fingers of June clouds teased the sun. It shone brighter than iridescent angel wings.

The violet-blue blossoms of the jacaranda trees that lined the driveway welcomed the guests.

Carriages drove past the trees to park in front of the hacienda. The cream-colored walls and the deep-red tile roof accented by brackets of golden bougainvillea blossoms smiled their welcome.

The excitement of human voices anticipated that something great was about to happen, my baptism.

The outside patio's tile floor was a glaze of reds, blues, and yellows, like a field of wildflowers. Guests were invited to sit at tables shaded by overhanging roofs. Wine was served.

In the middle of the patio, a fountain shot up a six-foot jet of water. Several two-foot jets accompanied it. Together they made a soft bubbling sound that muffled the sounds of conversation.

Ladies waved their fans to cool their faces and to draw attention to their eyes. Their mantillas flowed from their high hair combs, like lace masterpieces.

Some people mentioned the padre. "Was he late? Did something happen to him?"

The tinkle of small bells sounded. People arose. The red cassocks and white lace surplices of the altar servers caught everyone's attention. Behind the server carrying the processional cross walked the bowed figure of Padre Arturo. His white hair caught the sunlight and glowed like a halo. Guests lined up and followed him into the chapel.

My father accompanied Safira, who held me. Five pairs of godparents stood with us at the cream-colored marble baptismal font.

In the first row, my aunts and uncles sat with my eight-year-old brother, Christabo. My brother's face reflected a personal darkness. His eyes resented all the attention given to me. Attention that had been all his until I came along.

My godparents all took turns holding me. I was passed from one set to another until I came to my principal godparents.

Padre Arturo Gomez raised his hands over me. Then in a quiet voice, he began the words of the holy baptismal ceremony. He came to my anointing with the holy oil. I smiled. He came to put salt on my tongue. I flinched at its salty taste. Then came the moment of truth. He held a pink shell full of holy water over my forehead. He paused. Everyone leaned forward to hear the names bestowed on me. While pouring the water on me, Padre Arturo said, "I baptize you Maria, Josephina, Constancia, Mercedes, Felicia. In the name of the Father and of the Son and of the Holy Spirit. Amen."

All guests applauded politely. Christabo frowned.

My father smiled and quietly added, *Jacaranda*.

My mother, Safira, made the sign of the cross on herself and added, *Safira*. She also added her special Gypsy saint's name, Saint Sarah.

Jacaranda is my father's pet name for me. I have one black-brown eye from my mother and one jacaranda tree blossom's violet-blue eye from him.

The guests returned to the patio. They sat at tables laden with meats, vegetables, salads, sweets, and wine. They ate their fill from golden plates bearing the Moreno Gonzales coat of arms.

Guitar music and Gypsy voices singing songs of hope for all filtered down from the oak tree grove to the patio. It soothed and entertained the well-fed guests. Safira rocked my cradle and hummed her Gypsy lullabies to me.

Our Gypsies relaxed in the shade of our oak trees. They loosened their belts. If they wore shoes, they took them off. Their soft music soothed their hard-worked bodies. The lingering fragrance of good food and wine filled their senses. They relaxed. Some of the girls started to dance. Their slow beginning beat became a swirling of skirts. Legs, arms, and hips moved as the tempo increased. The *click, click, click* of the castanets added new meaning to the eyes of each dancer. The faded colors of their dresses received new life from the dance movements and the dappled sunlight shining through the oak trees.

The Gypsies had a secret. They smiled to themselves, knowing that I was one of them on my mother's side.

A small boy walked onto the patio. He was about seven or eight years old. He was different.

His hair and skin were almost white. His eyes were pink. He was an albino. Reaching out with his hands, speaking not a word, he asked for food.

With his arms full of food, he started to leave. He never ate in front of us. We never knew what he did with the food. Did he share it? He left. But Christabo followed him to a place behind the barn. We heard a strong neighing from the horses. Hooves stamped on pavement.

Christabo came out from behind the barn alone. He walked to the chapel.

Later, Safira looked into the chapel. She found streaks of blood mixed with the baptismal water.

We never saw the albino boy again.

CHAPTER 2

How quickly twelve years passed.

Jacaranda bloomed.

Shadows lurked on the full moon's face.

Did weddings bring hope?

The horse barn was Grast's home. The horses were his friends. Yes, he was the old Rom, a Gypsy, my closest friend. He taught me to ride by the age of six. I could outride and outrace anyone. Grast's great love for horses and people outshone his clawed left hand and scarred face.

My twenty-year-old brother, Christabo, beat his horse, Diablo, to a bloody pulp. All he knew was to whip, whip, whip with hate.

Eclipse was my new horse, a blue-black Arabian stallion. I trained him with carrots and lots of love. I've never owned a whip.

Safira taught all her Romany, Gypsy language and customs to me. I loved her folktales.

My father had already picked out my future husband, Henrique Morales. His father owned the ranchero next to ours, five thousand acres. It was a bit smaller than my father's.

When Henrique and Christabo went swimming in our lake, I spied. His *bicho* was larger than Christabo's. I smiled.

Later that morning, Christabo and I rode our horses down to the Guadalete River. The sand and the water were just right for a relaxing ride.

I smiled at my brother and cried, "I'll dare you."

"What'll you dare?"

"To race you back to the barn."

"Oh! Yes, yes, yes!"

"OK, get ready. Get set. Go!"

Our horses leapt into the air like tigers after a stag. My black-red hair danced in the wind with Eclipse's blue-black mane like lovers on fire. We were one.

Christabo led. I allowed him to lead. Otherwise he might quit.

As soon as I saw the barn, I patted Eclipse's neck and whispered in his ear, "Now, my love, run!"

As we passed an astonished Christabo and Diablo, I smiled out of my brother's whip length.

He frowned. His whip cut Diablo's neck and hindquarters. The more he whipped, the slower Diablo ran.

Grast greeted Eclipse and me with open arms.

"Hey, Jacaranda wins again," he cried. "Steady. Steady. I'll calm Eclipse and put him in his stall."

"Thank you, Grast." I dismounted.

"You sure know how to get the best of your brother. Look at him whippin' poor Diablo."

"Yes. He's cruel to animals and to people."

"I'll bring Eclipse to his stall. Hold your brother here until I get back. Let him cool off."

"OK. I'll try." I watched as Grast walked Eclipse to the barn.

Christabo arrived and grimaced, "You won."

"Yes. Thanks to Eclipse."

"It's Grast's fault."

"What?" I cried.

"He failed. If he had fed and groomed Diablo the way he should have, I would have won."

As Grast came out of the barn, Christabo glared at him. His dust-covered face and red eyes promised hate.

"You son of a Gypsy," swore my brother. "Get over here. Kneel. Give me your back so that I can dismount on you."

Grast lowered himself, going down on his hands and knees beside Diablo. He closed his eyes and clenched his muscles, waiting for Christabo's heavy feet and whip. The feet came first.They dug hard, like crab claws into butter. Then the whip lashed on his back, legs, and arms, again and again.

"Stop! Stop your cruelty!" I cried. "Grast has not harmed you."

"He's nothin' but a stinkin' Gypsy."

"Grast is a human being. That's more than I can say for you."

Christabo stopped. He left Diablo standing in his blood and sweat. My brother walked toward the hacienda. I ran and tackled him. Like a bag of *cagajon* (wastes), he hit the dust. I straddled him. With my hands on my hips, I laughed. The red-faced *cagado* (milksop) slithered from between my legs and ran to the hacienda.

"You will catch hell," Grast cried.

"He'd better watch out," I cried. My father taught me how to kick him in his *cajones* (glands) if he gets smart with me.

Grast bled from his cuts. He went and laid himself on his cot in the barn. I found soap and water to wash his wounds. Then I put salve on his cuts.

After a short rest, we took Diablo to his stall and nursed his wounds. We fed both horses.

Then I left to help with preparations for dinner in the hacienda.

Grast stayed in the barn by himself, or so he thought. At first, he heard a slight rustling noise in the straw next to the horse stalls. Then a mysterious whistling from nowhere and everywhere tickled his ears. He tried to turn away from the tantalizing sounds, thinking that it was only his imagination teasing him. Suddenly, he felt two hands grab his shoulders from behind and turn him around. He was face-to-face with a smiling Safira.

"Oh ho!" he cried, grabbing her waist and lifting her over his head.

"Chumide ma," she pleaded. Kiss me.

He put her down. "Now, Safira, don't get us into trouble with the senor."

"He's a *dilo kar* [stupid penis]! Most of the time he's *mato* [drunk]." She spit on the ground.

Then she looked at him straight in the eyes. "I'll be swimmin' in the lake *nango* [naked]."

Grast grabbed her right wrist with his clawed left hand. With his good right hand, he unsheathed his hunting knife. With a single slash, he nicked both of their palms. Their blood mingled. Now they were one Romany, Gypsy style.

Four years passed. At sixteen years of age, I was ready for my engagement party with Henrique.

On that special eve, as peons and Gypsies helped to finish the patio decorations, Grast, sitting on a barrel of red wine, thrust his twisted left hand high into the twilight air. He despised the overhanging garlands of paper flowers and candlelit paper lanterns.

They'll pluck the eyes out of a fartin' pig to outdo any other family's shasto *[party],* mused Grast. Making with a quick spit of tobacco juice, he smiled. *Why do people get so riled up?* He spat again. *Does Jaca want all this* dilimos *[stupidity]? That convent finishin' school must have planted a lot of high-class ideas into her practical country brain.* He spat again and rubbed a stubborn glob of thick dark-brown saliva from his bewhiskered chin.

Look at the old senor wavin' a bottle of brandy with his left fist and scratchin' his bul *[posterior] with his eatin' hand,* chuckled Grast. *He's three sheets to the wind but calls out orders like an old sea captain.*

Safira followed her senor, correcting his blunders with kind looks and resolving a mad man's serious concern for their daughter's engagement party.

Grast twitched his nose and took another swig of rum.

Night arrived. Carriages drove past the violet-blue blossoms of the jacaranda-tree-lined drive. They stopped at the hacienda's main entrance.

Christabo greeted each arrival. His false smile disguised his envy and hatred for all his father's friends.

I'll see old Chris rot in hell. Grast winced.

The next guest, Padre Fernando Salmanez, was the grand inquisitor for Cádiz, Spain. He was a cousin of the deceased Senora Margarita. Christabo fondled and kissed his cousin's right hand with exaggerated reverence and fear.

That Padre kills more people with a flick of his little finger than Chris can count the number of angels standin' on the head of a pin, mumbled Grast. *I hope he catches his death of somethin' painful, like the bite from an inquisitor's black cobra.* He brushed the hair out of his eyes with his left hand. *He's killed and tortured many of my Gypsy friends. He hung some on trees. Others he burned at the stake. He would kill me too if the senor did not keep us Gypsies safe to work on his ranchero.*

In the patio, the guitars and violins played for my engagement party. I relished the many-colored skirts and mantillas whirling together like a symphony of flowers. The senors pranced like brawny black bulls with clicking heals.

The party's gettin' wild, smiled Grast. *Jaca has her intended by his shirttail.*

I've already cooked Henrique's goose.

I danced with him. My white silk dress with lace ruffles floated in time with my black-red hair crowned with a tall ivory comb holding my long white lace mantilla.

The musicians played. The guests ate and drank. At two o'clock in the morning, the music lingered.

Grast mused as he watched the senor cuddle up to Safira, *Doesn't he know that she's my wife now?*

My intended and I danced under the stars. The early morning breeze cooled our warm bodies.

Grast thought, *There's a lot of Safira's blood in her movements.* He glanced at Safira again.

He caught her expression of joy for her daughter's happiness. *I hope she's pleased. Jaca's intended's a wealthy landowner's son. He's not a poor Gypsy like me.*

The wind blew faster. One of the paper flowers fell into a lantern's candle flame. The wind carried the flame from garland to garland. A wild fire blazed. Grast stood up, waving his rum bottle, shouting, *"Fire! Fire! Fire!"*

The flaming paper bits fell on us. My gown caught fire. I pulled my comb out of my hair and wrapped my mantilla around it. I used it to beat out the flames on my dress.

Henrique froze with eyes of fear. I cried to him for help. He walked away dumbfounded.

Safira cried out loud, "Saint Sarah, save my child!"

The guests tried to help one another. Some found water to douse the flames. Others wadded up their shawls to smother flames on themselves and others. The disaster brought out the best in most of the people.

My dress became a wet mess. My father and Safira came to my aid. They patted my hair and gown with wet rags torn from their own clothing. They cried aloud, "Please, God, save *our daughter*!"

Grast heard their prayer. He gasped. *They do not know what they are saying!*

I thanked my father and Safira for their help. I helped the guests nearest to me.

After all the flames were out, the people pulled themselves together and went home.

I thanked God that no one was seriously hurt.

I saw Grast glare at Christabo.

Christabo had an evil glint in his eyes. He had heard my father's and Safira's prayer.

Grast thought, *What can I do to prevent a tragedy?* He smashed his rum bottle against the tile floor. He flashed the jagged bottle neck and thought, *That ought to take care of Chris!* Then he watched Christabo walk over to his cousin Padre Fernando. They whispered.

"Oh no!" gasped Grast.

The smiles on the two cousins' faces turned into stygian grins.

Of all the guests, only Padre Fernando remained. Quietly he pointed his skinny right forefinger at me. With odium, he whispered, "You are a *Gypsy*!" He turned his ashen face toward Safira and released his threat. "You, Gypsy, and your adulterous senor and your bastard shall all *burn at the stake*." He turned to Christabo, who escorted him to his carriage.

We looked at one another. No one spoke a word. We went to our rooms.

I wondered, *What could be in store for me as a Gypsy*? I did not know this horrible secret about myself until I was about to marry the man I did not love.

CHAPTER 3

Prison cells stifled freedom.

Fires burned bodies.

Thoughts roamed free forever and ever.

Hopefulness survived.

Our trials were short. My father, my mother, and I were to be burned at the stake.

From my prison cell window, I could see the downtown plaza in Cádiz where we would all be burned alive.

I shared my cell with a blind girl, Catalina. She was about my age. Her eyes had been put out with a red-hot branding iron. Her torturers tried to make her name other lapsed Catholics. She refused. Her family was Jewish. All Jews and Moors were given a choice: become Catholic or leave Spain.

Her family was very wealthy. They chose to stay and become Catholic on the outside. The Inquisition coveted their wealth. Spies accused them of celebrating Judaism in secret. Her parents have been burned at the stake. She would be next.

"In darkness, the blind see no walls," said Catalina to me.

She made me realize, *It's walls, material and mental, that keep people apart.*

Unable to see physically, she focused on sound, smell, taste, and touch to communicate.

She heard the mice nibbling on her straw mattress. The crunching sound pleased and comforted her with the thought that something, even a mouse, seemed happy living in prison.

"Listen to the mice, Jacaranda. The Inquisition doesn't worry them. All they care about is something to eat and a place to sleep."

I smiled.

She felt the warmth of my smile, like the flame of a small candle. "Oh, to be a mouse! Nobody hunts them for heresy."

I took her hand in mine and kissed her fingers.

"Thank you. I believe you are a kind person. If all Catholics were as kind as you are, I'd like to become one."

"We are all God's children. Our father Abraham and his sons, Ishmael and Isaac, started our family as numerous as the stars and the grains of sand. Jesus taught us to love one another."

"I love you."

"And I love you. God gives us the grace to follow his plan for us, each in his own way."

Suddenly, the noise of a crowd of people erupted outside our cell window. I looked out. The church bells sounded the noon Angelus. The rain began to blur my vision of the plaza.

The crowd yelled and hooted above the sound of the bells. They jeered at someone dressed in a yellow garment. The victim wore a tall cylindrical yellow paper hat. The word *heretic* was written on it in big red letters. In the rain, the victim looked like my father. "*Father! Father!*" I cried and wept. I could no longer see through my tears and the rain.

"There, there," whispered Catalina. "Cry all the tears that you can. I can't cry anymore. You'll have to cry for the both of us."

"My father wasn't perfect. But he was kind to me and the Gypsies."

"Yes, I believe you."

"They're tying him to the stake."

"Yes. They did the same to my mother and father."

"He looks so helpless."

"Yes. Pray for him. Say your prayers and I'll say mine."

"Thank you, Catalina."

"I hear him shouting something. Can you understand him?"

"Yes. He's praying his favorite prayer, Jesus, Son of God, have mercy on me, a sinner."

"He's shouting it over and over again."

I prayed, "O Jesus, have mercy on him." I watched the flames and smoke engulfing my father's body, hiding him from my sight. I wished that I could have been blinded like Catalina. She could not see this horror.

Night came with a cover of clouds. A light rain fell. I rested on my straw mattress. But my mind could not blot out this day's horror.

After my eyes closed and my mind cleared, a tiny knocking noise tickled my ears. I rubbed my ears. The noise did not go away. *Was it that darned mouse? No. Was it Catalina? No.* There, it happened again. It was slightly louder this time. It seemed to be coming from the cell window or from some place outside the window. I got up. I went to the window.

The rain and the darkness hid everything. The tapping happened again. It came from a place below the window on the outside wall. I pressed my face against the bars to look down on the outside wall. My eyes discovered the dark figure of a man. He was knocking on the wall.

"Who are you?" I called.

"Speak softly. You'll wake the police. It's me, Grast."

"I don't believe you. The inquisitors hung all our ranchero's Gypsies. How could you escape?"

"I hid under our lake's water with a straw for breathing."

"You'd better hide or they'll hang you too."

"I've come to rescue you."

"Don't make me laugh. How can you get me out of this cell?"

"We Gypsies have a secret. We helped build this prison. And we constructed the cell's window bars according to our secret Gypsy plans."

"Oh."

"Yes. Lift up one of those bars."

I lifted up one of the bars. It rose up out of the bottom hole. "You're right." Then I pulled the bar down and out of the top hole. "Eureka." In no time at all, I pulled out all the bars.

"Now, climb out, and I'll help you down."

"Wait. I have a friend here. She needs to be saved too, or she'll be burned at the stake."

"All right. But tell her to be quick."

Turning to the sleeping Catalina, I whispered, "Wake up. Grast is here to save us."

Rubbing her face, she murmured, "Don't fool me."

"No fooling. He has opened the window for us to get out. He's below to bring us to a safe place."

"But I can't see. I'll be a burden."

"Nonsense. Come on, or would you prefer to burn at the stake?"

"No. I'll go." She arose and felt her way to the window.

I lifted her, feet first, out the window. Then with her hands grabbing the windowsill, she lowered herself into Grast's arms. I followed.

"She's blind."

"I know. But she's alert and able to use her other senses better than we can."

"We need someone like that."

"I knew you'd understand. Where are you taking us?"

"I've a special place down by the harbor."

"Great," I said. Then turning to Catalina, I whispered, "Take my hand and follow me."

Grast grabbed my arm. "First, lift me up to the window so that I can reset the bars. We do not want the police to know our Gypsy secret."

Catalina and I got down on our hands and knees. Grast stood on our backs and replaced the bars. "There. They'll think the angels opened the gates and let you out." He jumped down.

Then we walked fast in the rain to our place of safety.

"Welcome to our Gypsy hideaway," smiled Grast, lighting a small candle. "Now, I'll change you fine young ladies into fine young Gypsy lads. The police chopped off your hair for the stake. I'll shave it all off for your safety."

"What? Never!" I yelled.

"Oh yes!" shouted Grast. As he continued to flash a long razor blade in his right hand and a cup of shaving suds in his other hand, he laughed, "You'll need it for your total transformation process. After this comes the dark coloring for your skin."

"What's wrong with our skin?" I dared to ask.

"It's too light for a Gypsy lad." Then he cocked his head and smiled. "Didn't Safira tell you how we Gypsies got our beautiful skin color?"

"No."

"Well, one day, God was making his first human being. He made a beautiful human figure in clay. He was very pleased with his masterpiece. So he put it in the oven to bake. Then he started to make another human being and forgot the time to take the first one out of the oven. Suddenly, he smelled something burning. He opened the oven and there was his first human being burnt to a crisp. But alive. So he took that human being out of the oven and loved it with all his heart.

"Then he put the next clay figure into his oven. He started to make another clay figure. But this time, he remembered about the timing. He counted the minutes so quickly on his fingers that he finished counting before the figure was properly cooked. He opened the oven door, and behold, the figure was a pale, undone human being. But it moved. It was alive. So he held it in his hands and loved it with all his heart.

"Finally, he placed his third clay figure into the oven. He sat in front of the oven and counted his fingers properly for the proper baking time. Then he opened the oven door. And lo and behold, there was his figure, a beautiful golden brown. It was alive and smiling. God took it into his hands and loved it with all his heart. This was his first Gypsy."

Catalina sat smiling at both of us.

"What's funny?" I asked.

"You both sound like my mother and father having a good Jewish argument."

"This is only the beginning," chimed Grast. "Now prepare your heads for the action."

He stroked his blade back and forth on the razor strop. Then he began the shaving—first me, then Catalina.

The walnut juice came next. I wondered just how far he intended to go. Did he intend it to cover some or all the parts of our body?

"We'll be as modest as we can be for both of you," added Grast. "Jaca, you can stain Catalina all over her body behind the screen in the corner over there. Then do as much of your own body as you can reach. Then lie facedown on your prison smock and I'll do the rest."

I couldn't think of anything to say. It was like he was grooming his horses back at our barn.

After doing Catalina and the front of myself, I cried out, "Grast, I'm all yours."

Finally, Catalina and I were golden-brown Gypsy lads from the top of our heads to the souls of our feet.

Next, Grast handed boy's underwear to us over the screen. We donned it.

Then he produced a large ragbag of clothing. "Choose whatever suits your fancy."

I selected a pair of large dark-blue pantaloons, brown sandals, a loose dark-green shirt with full sleeves, and a very roomy dark-gray jacket that came down to my knees. I could never be recognized as a girl by any stretch of anyone's imagination. I picked out a similar outfit for Catalina. Then we came out from behind the screen.

Grast gasped. "Well done." Then he went to another box of items and pulled out three eye patches. "Here's two for Catalina and one for you, Jaca."

"My eyes are all right. Why do I need this?"

"You have a pair of different-colored eyes, one violet blue and one black brown. To be a Gypsy, you need to cover the violet-blue one."

"Now, you look great. But do you smell right?"

"Smell?" I said. "What's to smell?"

"You," Grast replied. "You must have the foul Gypsy smell for the people who hate us."

"I smell you," Catalina sputtered. "You smell fresh and clean."

"Exactly," replied Grast. "We like to be clean, to take baths and smell like roses. But most non-Gypsies, *Gazhos*, who hate us, expect us to be filthy and stink."

"What's that new terrible smell?" cried Catalina.

"I've just opened a special box of Gypsy-hater smells," mused Grast. "This is how Gypsy haters expect us to smell." He handed a small pouch on a long neck cord to each of us. "Put it around your neck and under your shirt. When people smell this, they'll do anything to get rid of you. To activate it, just dip it in water. Dry, it will not smell."

I said, "You did not use this on the ranchero."

"You and your father—may God rest his soul in peace—and others, except Christabo, didn't think of us as stinking Gypsies."

Grast pulled another box from the back shelf. "Now here's another important item, a black leather glove."

"What's so special about that?" I said. "It looks just like any other glove to me."

"It looks the same outside. But it's the inside that counts."

"How does it count?" asked Catalina.

"Inside it is lined with small sharp pieces of broken glass," said Grast. He demonstrated by turning the glove inside out and putting it on his hand. "See." The glass pieces stood out from the palm and fingers of his hand. "You could scratch your opponent's eyes out or cut his throat with one swipe of your hand." He removed the glove and turned it right side out again.

"Keep this in the inside pocket of your coat."

"You bet!" Catalina and I replied.

"Now, most Gypsies, like me, have never been to fancy schools like you ladies. So you must act like you cannot read or write."

"Yes," we echoed together.

"But you can read secretly, without letting anyone know. When it's to our advantage."

Then with a sly smile, Grast pulled another box from the bottom shelf. "This next item is very special to hide your feminine identity." He uncovered a small, six-inch metal funnel. It was flat. But with a quick press of his fingers, it opened full and round. "This will be your male organ. With it, in its proper place, you can pee on any alley wall, standing up, just like any of us gentlemen."

"Wow!" We blushed, putting our flattened funnels inside our coat pockets. We could not think of another word to say.

"Now, go to sleep. Tomorrow is a busy day. Safira will be burned at the stake."

"Can we save her?" I hoped.

"Maybe," replied Grast, blowing out the candle.

"Will I ever get used to that horrible smell?" asked Catalina.

At sunrise, we awakened. I rinsed my face and hands in a basin of cold water. I looked into a piece of broken mirror over the washbasin. The walnut stain had not budged. My face remained a new golden brown.

Already, Grast was washed. He had even cooked eggs and sausages for our breakfast.

"Good morning, lads."

"Same to you," we replied with full mouths.

"What can we do for Safira?" I asked.

"I'm still thinking about that," Grast replied.

"It's still raining," I observed while washing the dishes.

"We'll just have to pray for her," suggested Catalina.

"Jaca, put on that floppy hat and come with me to the town square."

"Sure."

"Just a minute. You must have lad's names. Jaca, we'll call you Jaco. And Catalina, we'll call you Cato."

"Thank you for reminding us, Grast," I replied. Catalina nodded.

"I'll help my wife any way I can," promised Grast.

"You'll have all my best Jewish prayers," promised Catalina.

"Take good care of this place, Cato. Jaco, let's go."

The town square was crowded with people anxious to see a Gypsy burn at the stake.

I saw hate in their faces.

The wooden fagots were laid out from the stake so that the victim would suffer and choke from the smoke before being consumed by the flames.

The inquisitors were seated in their grandstand opposite the stake. I saw Padre Fernando Salmanez, a Harpy, sharpening his claws. What surprised me was Christabo sitting next to him, wearing the garb of a novice monk.

Grast edged us up to a place in the crowd behind the stake. We waited for the guards to bring Safira to the stake.

"Whatever happens, don't move from this spot," Grast warned me.

As Safira appeared, surrounded by guards, the crowd jeered her.

"Down with all the good-for-nothing Gypsies."

Some threw rocks at her. One rock grazed her forehead. She began to bleed. She walked barefoot, wearing the yellow garb and the tall paper hat of a heretic. When she reached the stake, her guards tied her with ropes so that she could not move.

Grast looked at his wife. Tears filled his eyes.

Safira looked up to the sky. She prayed aloud, "Saint Sarah, pray for me, a sinner!" Over and over she shouted, "Saint Sarah, pray for me, a sinner!"

The guards received the signal from Padre Fernando to light the wooden fagots. Flames and smoke filled the air. I could only see the faint silhouette of Safira.

Then I saw Grast climbing through the burning fagots to reach his wife. I heard him say, "My dear wife, I'll strangle you before the flames burn one inch of your precious body."

Safira continued her prayer, "Saint Sarah, have mercy on me, a sinner."

All of a sudden, huge storm clouds gathered over the town square. Lightning flashed. Thunder roared. The grandstand collapsed. Padre Fernando and Christabo fled. The people trampled over one another. Confusion reigned.

Another bolt of lightning hit the stake, untying the ropes and freeing Safira. Rain poured, extinguishing the fire. I saw two figures descend from the stake. One was carrying the other. Grast held Safira in his arms. She had fainted.

"Let's go to our hideout," whispered Grast.

"I want to cover Safira with my jacket," I cried.

"Yes. We need to cover the yellow garment."

The heavy rain continued. It helped to conceal us. Soon we reached our hideaway.

Catalina heard us sloshing in the mud. She opened the door. We stumbled into our safe place.

"Fix that mattress," pleaded Grast. "Get warm water and a clean cloth to wash Safira."

I brought the washbasin full of warm water. Catalina removed the yellow garment of shame. Then we washed the unconscious body. Soon, an arm and a hand moved.

Safira opened her eyes and whispered, "Where am I?"

"You're safe," Grast said softly, kissing her hand and rubbing her arm for warmth.

"Thank you, Saint Sarah," prayed Safira. Then she smiled at all of us. She looked at Catalina and me with mysterious eyes. "Do I know you? Tell me, Grast. Who are these young men?"

"This one with the one eye patch is Jaca, your daughter. And the other with two eye patches is her former cell mate, Catalina. Their disguise names are Jaco and Cato. Their disguise will help them to be safe from pawing sailors' hands aboard ship. Tomorrow we'll look for a passage to New Spain."

"First," bellowed Safira, "I'll tell them something about themselves as women."

"We know how to protect ourselves," I mused. "Grast gave us his glass-lined gloves to ward off our attackers."

"My advice is about being the best woman for the best man that you may meet someday."

"We're all ears," chimed Jaca and Catalina together.

"This is an old trick that I learned from a Moorish elder woman. She learned to belly dance as a young girl. The tents that she lived in were three to four feet high. So she danced on her knees. The dancing tightened up her muscles, beginning with her *gi* [stomach], her *pulpa* [thigh], her *butuko* [buttock], and her *mizh* [vagina]. Without using her fingers, she learned to pick up a nine-inch stack of coins with her *mizh* muscles. By developing this particular muscle group, she could play Beethoven's Ninth Symphony on any *goro*'s [male wretch's] *kar* [penis]."

"Who's Beethoven?" mumbled Grast.

"My *dikhel ando suno* [my second sight] tells me that he will be born in Germany in 1770 and compose nine beautiful symphonies."

"You get my *buzno* [goat] with your *drabarimaski patrin* [fortune cookies]," chuckled Grast.

"Wait until I get your *kar*. Then you'll know the Ninth Symphony's famous *dah, dah, dah boom*!"

"Thank you," whistled Catalina and I.

Grast smiled.

I went to sleep that night exercising my muscles.

CHAPTER 4

Seagulls winged on ocean air.

Galleons sailed on,

New Spain sweet-talked adventurers.

Sirens sang scam songs.

The next day, Grast and I explored the harbor. We saw many galleons lying about, waiting for the right wind and tide to sail to some exotic destination. Having no pesos, we hoped to work our way to New Spain.

Several ships had full crews. Finally, we spotted a beautiful galleon, *La Aguila*, square-rigged on the foremast and mainmast and lateen-rigged on the two aftermasts. The creamy-white sails were enhanced by huge red crosses. I did not know what country the yellow-and-red flag represented. We crossed our fingers and went aboard.

A man wearing a black buccaneer hat with a long red feather trailing over his left shoulder grimaced at us with sharp black eyes and tight thin lips. "I'm Lupe Gonzales, the crew master. What can I do for you gentlemen?"

I was intrigued by his long red feather.

Grast spoke, "Good sir, will you hire four hands willing to work their way to New Spain?"

"We have need for cooks and cargo men," Lupe replied.

"There are four of us. Two can cook and two can do cargo," bargained Grast.

"Hired. Be here tomorrow at dawn." Eyeing the patch over my left eye, Lupe asked, "Are you a pirate?"

"No," I replied. "We're Gypsies."

"Work hard, or overboard you go."

"We always work hard, eh, Jaco?" chuckled Grast.

"Absolutely!" I agreed. Looking around, I saw the men working on the deck and in the riggings. All looked in shipshape. But from one of the cargo holes came a strange stench.

"What's your cargo?" I asked.

"At present, we have slaves from West African ports for plantation owners in New Spain," smiled Lupe. His red feather trembled in the wind.

I looked at Grast. He looked at me and mumbled, "*Manai love. Manai alomos.*" No money. No choice.

"We'll set sail tomorrow morning at high tide," warned Lupe. "Be here at dawn."

"Yes, sir," we replied. Then we hurried back to share the news with Safira and Catalina.

At dawn, the four of us boarded *La Aguila.* Safira and Catalina, now recognized by her new masculine name, Cato, were taken to the galley as cook's helpers.

Grast and I, now going by my masculine nickname, Jaco, were assigned to the cleanup crew. Hammocks were assigned. Fellow shipmates were met. Some were uglier than rotten potatoes. Others had a mischievous sneer on one eye or the lower lip that dared anyone to cross them. The worst of all was a horrible, scar-faced creature with a patch over his right eye and a bum left leg. He called himself Corte.

"All hands on deck!" shouted Lupe.

We all rushed to attention on the main deck.

Lupe stepped up to the poop deck railing and, glaring down at us with his ratlike eyes, proclaimed with a generous gesture of his open right hand to the man on his right. "Gentlemen, this is your captain, the most honorable Captain Jose Moralez. Do your work well and there will be no trouble. One word of insolence or act of disobedience and it will be chains and the whip. Now, go to your stations and prepare to sail to New Spain for God and our king."

We all raised our hands high above our heads and shouted, "Hooray, hooray, hooray for God and our king!"

Lupe continued with a smile like a calculating lion, "Now, our voyage should take four to six weeks. Providing, of course, that the weather is fair and, of course, that we are not attacked by pirates." He paused and then questioned, "Are there any questions?"

We all knew better than to ask any questions.

"Dismissed!" shouted Lupe.

Grast and I started to climb the rigging for the mainmast to let out the sails. Some of the crew began to sing a sailor's chantey to keep time as they worked. Good will and happy thoughts prevailed. But what would six or more weeks bring?

Lupe, like a lion ready to leap, yelled, "Grast and Jaco, get down and head for the cargo bays! Attend our cargo of slaves. Feed and clean them. They'll need to be in good condition to get the best price at the slave market at Port San Sabastiano in New Spain."

"Yes, sir!" we replied. Like a flash of lightning, we descended. Our eyes accustomed themselves to the darkness as we climbed down into the cargo hole with its choking stench of helpless human beings.

I could not have believed the inhuman misery of the slaves. Row after row of men, boys, and women chained to their bed of wooden planks. Most of them were completely naked. Some wore a soiled breechcloth. They were all lying in their own and their neighbors' filth of urine and excrement.

Grast handed a bucket of water and a bar of soap to me. Together, we walked to the nearest victim. Without a word, we began washing each person as a brother, as a sister, as a human being.

After washing and breech-clothing the first row of people, Grast began to hum a Gypsy song. Soon, some of the people joined in with him. Some sang the words "I know a Gypsy in Cádiz. His dear wife he loved. Like a nightingale she sang. True love conquers all."

I hummed and cleaned. Our work went faster and faster. Grast discovered that some of the people were Gypsies from the west coast of Africa.

Safira and Catalina brought bread, fried fish, and water. They helped each person to eat a healthy meal.

Grast smiled at Safira and said, "You are doing a fine job feeding these unfortunate people. Some of them are Gypsies like us."

We like working in the galley. One old man with a patch over his right eye winks at Catalina. She can't see his wink, but she feels it and blushes. He calls himself Corte because his face is so cut up with scars his mother wouldn't recognize him. He came from a prison in Cádiz. He says that prisoners have been given a choice, either work on ships going to New Spain or rot in prison.

Catalina felt her way to a woman prisoner and began massaging her arms and back. Other prisoners asked her to help them too. Grast and I began to massage the men. We all sang or hummed Grast's song, "True Love."

CHAPTER 5

Ship's shadows obscured dark thoughts.

Deep dreams revived hope.

Between flying red sails and steady green keels,

Crews worked and slept tight.

In the crew's sleeping quarters, I called to Catalina. "Hello. Are you ready for a good night's rest?"

"You might be, but not I," moaned Catalina. "All the night noises keep me awake."

"What noises?" I asked.

"Just the normal sleeping noises of the crew."

"Oh, they're just human beings making human sounds."

"Yes, but why do they have to be sooo human?"

"It's a way to get to know each one better without them knowing it."

"I know how they smell, especially when they pass gas."

"A good flatulence is very normal and can reveal a lot more than a smell. Think of the musical side of one's flatus. Old Skinny Bones, the captain's first mate, gives off with a wheezing *toot toot toot* that tells me he loves to tango."

"You've got a fantastic imagination, Jaco. Old Skinny Bones would have a hard time tangoing with his wooden leg."

"Think of Red Feather Lupe when he lets go with a thunderous *boom, boom, boom gazoom*. That tells me how much he dreams of his crafty old mother-in-law."

"What does Enrico el Fresco conjure up with his *put, put* whistle?"

"Why, he's mad at the world."

"And the world's mad at him," sighed Catalina

"How can you be so certain? Maybe he's just hard to understand. His thoughts just don't come out of his mouth as well as they do in his flatus." I turned around to catch a glimpse of Grast coming toward us. "Here comes Grast. I'll bet that he knows a lot more than we do about men's gas."

"Hi, you two, what makes you look so serious?" asked Grast with questioning eyes.

I replied, "We're considering the hidden meanings behind our crew members' gaseous explosions at night when they sleep."

"Oh," considered Grast. "Do you mean their *khai* [Rom for the inaudible] or their *rril* [Rom for the loud release] of human gas explosions? We Gypsy Rom prefer the *rril*. It proclaims us as a real human being."

"I suppose," inquired Cato, "that the *khai* is preferred by lady Roms?"

"Oh yes!" mused Grast. "They have many skirts to muffle the sound, but they enjoy a good blast of gas once in a while to get their point across to us men."

"Well," I proposed, "the men's pants are too thin to muffle a great intestinal gaseous manifestation?"

"Quite so," agreed Grast. "But if the Rom stands too close to any fire, his intestinal gas release will explode into flames and give him away."

"Does Safira *khai* or *rril*?" I asked Grast.

"She sure does!" he replied with a sharp smile. "She uses both to hoodwink me."

"I heard that!" snapped Safira, walking her way into the sleeping quarters. "Whose business is it to know if I *khai* or *rril*?"

"We're discussing how much we can learn about a person from his or her unintentional human body noises," added Cato.

"Well, you must diagnose Grast's *xurimos* [Rom for *snoring*]. That will tell you many of his secrets," wheedled Safira as she hung up her hammock and arranged her blanket and pillow for a good night's sleep.

"It takes a real Gypsy Rom to *xurimos*," protested Grast.

"Jaco and Cato can learn a lot about *xurimos* and *rril* and *khai* from you," grinned Safira, climbing into her hammock for a good night's sleep. But her ears were busy on their own, listening to the noises of the sleeping men. Suddenly, there came an extraloud *rril* from the back of the sleeping quarters. There it came again, a singular sound surpassing all the other *rrils* in existence. Safira's ears perked up. A knowing sparkle fired up in her eyes. "I've heard that one before." She smiled. "It brings back bittersweet memories. It's impossible. The originator of that *rril* died at the stake two days before they tried to burn me."

Knitting his brows in question, Grast peered at his wife. His sad black eyes searched her face. "Whom do you mean?" he whispered.

She whispered back, "The senor, Jaca's father." Her hands flew above her head like doves fluttering in flight, unable to find a safe place to land.

I dropped my blanket onto the hammock and turned to Safira. I sobbed. "It wasn't my father."

"Yes, tell us what you know," sought Grast. His dark eyes pleaded for understanding. His clawed left hand reached out to soothe Safira's shuddering shoulders.

"That famous *rril* came from the ugliest sailor in our crew, Corte."

I snorted like an adolescent pollywog losing its tail.

"I know him from the galley," added Cato. "He let me feel his face one day. His scars are terrible. His right eye is blind. He wears a patch like me. He works in the galley, washing the big cooking pots. He's lame in his left leg from the torture he received in prison. I doubt if his mother would recognize him."

"Yes, I know him too," added Safira. "Without a word, he helps me. I feel kindness in his silence."

"Get into your sacks!" yelled a nearby husky voice.

"*Si, si*," volunteered Grast.

We all climbed into our hammocks. We swung to and fro, searching for sleep. Mighty *rrils* and humongous *xurimos* from our crewmates did their best to steal our sleep. In my dreams, I saw myself standing next to a campfire. Suddenly, a big flame flashed outside the back of my pants. I thought to myself, *Yes, Jacaranda, amidst the fragrance of forgotten fish, you are the light of the world.*

CHAPTER 6

Winds blew. Galleons sailed on.

After the sunrise,

Troubles boiled until all was red.

Hope died at sunset.

Three weeks have passed. Grast and I, Jacaranda or Jaco, have done our work well. The slaves are in tip-top condition for the slave market in New Spain.

But Lupe Gonzales noticed some guns and ammunition missing from the locked supply room. He organized a search party. They found three pistol balls and some powder hidden in Grast's hammock.

"Ahoy, Grast," called Lupe, "come up to the poop deck. The captain wants to speak with you."

"Yes, sir!" responded Grast. "I wonder what he wants." He scratched his chin with his withered left hand. His eyes registered a feeling of surprise. "Could he want to thank me for taking such good care of his human cargo?"

On the poop deck, the captain took out from his blue silk jacket pocket a gold snuffbox. With his back to the wind, he inhaled a whiff of the fragrant tobacco. He smiled. His eyes glanced at the stern-faced Lupe. Then his wondering eyes focused on the bewildered Grast. With a flip of his right hand, he rearranged the neck and chest ruffles of his white silk shirt, which had been disturbed by the brisk wind.

Lupe gave his sternest look to Grast. Two guards leered like birds of prey. Their slobbering wet lips dripped contempt toward Grast. Meanwhile, Grast stood at attention, contemplating what his reward might be. His Gypsy heart beat proudly. Now he was proud to be a Gypsy. The scar running down from his forehead to his left cheek glistened like red gold. His mind sizzled. *What will my reward be?*

"Ahem!" the captain growled. "What is all this about? Some ammunition has been found in your hammock."

Grast's mouth dropped open. His tongue fluttered like a lost hummingbird. "Ammunition?" He paused. "I know nothing about ammunition in my hammock." His facial scar turned black.

"However," added Lupe, "it was found there."

"There must be some mistake, sir," Grast pleaded. His eyes filled with tears. "I don't own a gun or any ammunition."

"Nevertheless," mused the captain, "some guns and ammunition have been taken from the locked supply room. I must make an example of you for all the crew to see." He paused. "You will receive twenty lashes of the cat-o'-nine-tails on your bare back at sunset today."

A dumbfounded Grast sputtered, "But . . . but . . . but . . . ?"

"No *buts*," cried Lupe. "Guards, put the prisoner in chains till sunset."

Chained against the ship's prison bulkhead, Grast waited for sunset.

Two other prisoners, chained near him, looked him over with a sly intent. The one with a large M-shaped purple scar in the middle of his forehead, the brand of a murderer, whispered, "What's your trouble, mate?"

"They found ammunition in my hammock," sighed Grast.

"Oho! You must be one of us pirates. My name's Dead Spot. What's yours?"

"I'm Grast. That's Gypsy for *horse*. I specialize in caring for horses. I'm a Gypsy, not a pirate."

"Well, Gypsies can be pirates too. We aint prejudiced. Anyone is welcome to piracy. Welcome to our club, Grast."

"Have you been stealing the guns and ammunition?" asked Grast.

The other prisoner, with the long braided red beard and hair, Hoopla by name, replied, "Yes. And our plan is to attack at sunset today."

"That's when I get my whipping," gasped Grast.

"You'll be our distraction," sighed Hoopla. "But we'll cut you down as soon as we take command of the galleon."

"How many are you?" asked Grast.

"About thirty. Lupe's our leader," replied Hoopla. "When he comes to take you, he'll free us."

"We have guns and swords," Dead Spot added. "We'll have a sword for you."

I entered the prison and spotted Grast fastened to the bulkhead. In a low voice, I asked, "What's happening? Safira's worried."

"I'm to be whipped at sunset today," responded Grast. "They found ammunition in my hammock."

"How did it get there?" I asked.

"Someone planted it, to trap me."

"Can I help?"

"No. At sunset, just stay in the galley with Safira and Cato. Don't come out. You'll hear a lot of commotion, even gunshots. But do not come out until I knock on the galley door."

"Yes. But Safira will want to know why."

"Tell her not to worry. Just to look into her crystal ball mind."

"Sure! But you know Safira."

As the sun began to set, I went to the galley. I found Safira, Cato, and Corte polishing the stove. "Stay put," I whispered. "Grast's orders. No questions."

Safira's mental eyes searched for a hidden meaning under Grast's words.

We all sat. The quiet became louder and louder.

Lupe and the two guards came down to the prison. The two guards led Grast up to the main deck. Lupe remained behind to free the two pirate prisoners.

On the main deck, under the shadow of the mainmast's square-rigged sails, Grast's wrists were tied high above his head to the mainmast. His shirt was ripped off his back. The red light of the sunset fired up his naked back waiting for the first lash of the cat-o'-nine-tails.

Lupe gave the signal, a sharp clap of his hands, to the drummer, who began the dreaded rolling sound of the drumsticks drumming against the tautest hide of the drum's head.

Rat-a-tat-tat . . . rat-a-tat-tat . . . rat-a-tat-tat.

Lupe gave a second signal, another sharp clap of his hands, to the large man with the cat-o'-nine-tails cradled in his crossed arms.

The large man slowly uncrossed his arms and raised the weapon in his right hand for the first slash of the cat-o'-nine-tails against Grast's waiting back.

But before that first slash came, Lupe raised his sword and drove its shining blue blade deep into the captain's white silk shirt and into his heart. The cat-o'-nine-tail's sharpened metal barbs never touched Grast's defenseless back flesh.

Dead Spot cut the rope holding Grast's wrists to the mainmast and handed him a sword. With a tooth-or-two-missing grin, he smiled at Grast and yelled, "Come on, fellow pirate!"

Hoopla shook his mighty red hair braids and cried, "You're one of us now. Fight like hell!"

Grast fought like a horse on fire. He dashed from one helpless sailor to another. He slashed his way, cutting arms and legs and necks until the decks ran red with blood. Then he came to the galley door. Rattling his sword against it, he yelled, "Let me in!"

Safira opened the door. Grast entered and closed the door. We sat. Mutiny's rancid smells and raucous sounds offended our sense of human dignity. We waited for God knows what!

Amid the victory shouts and pillaging, Lupe, now Captain Lupe Gonzales, raised the black-and-white flag of the skull and crossbones atop the mainmast. Then he came to the galley. With an oily smile, he addressed Safira, "Cook up some grub for our pirate crew." Then turning to all of us, he boasted, "You did a fantastic job. Welcome to piracy. Come topside and get your fill of rum and loot." Then putting his right arm around Grast's shoulders, he led us topside.

Rum was king. The pirates opened the barrels of rum. Splashing, they drank their fill. Grast and the rest of us, including Corte, played along. We pretended to drink. We sang drunkards' songs with gusto and swagger. We danced to the hornpipe with nimble feet, shuffling and kicking out of tune but keeping time with the drum and fife. Safira twirled her skirts. But not too high.

After the dead pirates and faithful crew members were stripped of their good clothing, jewelry, and any gold or silver teeth, they were thrown overboard to the sharks. Grast and I helped to clear the deck.

The next day, at midafternoon, the watchman on the crow's nest called, "Land ho!"

Some were too exhausted to wake up. Others fumbled around like newborn ponies trying to stand up. Grast and I looked west. We saw the distant, hazy blue-and-gold outline of New Spain.

"Look to the slaves," barked Lupe to Grast and me.

"Yes, sir!" we replied.

"See that they are all fresh and clean for the slave market when we arrive."

"Yes, sir!" we snapped sharply as we went below to prepare the slaves for the auction block.

La Aguila entered Port San Sabastiano at midmorning. The hands of the slaves were tied behind their backs. The slaves were tied to one another by a noose around their neck tied to a noose around each of their neighbor's neck.

"Drive 'em out!" yelled Lupe. Then turning to the guards, he said, "Tie up Grast, Safira, Jaco, Cato, and Corte. And add them to the rest of the slaves."

Before we could realize our destiny, we were tied up as slaves.

"Thought you leprous Gypsies could outsmart me?" teased Lupe. "I was on to your foolishness long ago. Now, you nonpersons will bring a fine price as slaves."

Dumbly we looked at one another. *I was in New Spain, but at what a price. I faked piracy. But how can I falsify slavery?* I raised my eyes to heaven. *Only God can help me now.*

The slaves began chanting Grast's deep song, first with a deep hum then with words:

Hum. "I know." Hum. "A Cádiz." Hum. "Gypsy." Hum. "His dear wife." Hum. "He." Hum. "Loved." Hum. "Like." Hum. "A nightingale." Hum. "She sang." Hum. "True." Hum. "Love." Hum. "Conquers." Hum. "All." Hum.

CHAPTER 7

Dark beginnings begged for hope.

We Gypsies dreamt dreams.

The sky served as our rooftop.

The earth was our home.

Port San Sabastiano opened its arms to welcome new faces, new ideas, new talents, and new pesos.

Pirate captain Lupe Gonzales led his rogue band and his cargo of us slaves ashore to dazzle and outwit the unsuspecting natives and the fortune-grasping immigrants of New Spain. He wore his new captain's uniform, a blue silk jacket and a ruffled white shirt with a sword hole, complete with bloodstains over his heart. He could be seen as one who has risen from the dead, but one who is to be feared rather than to be loved. Oh yes, he still sported his black buccaneer hat, with its long red feather trailing over his left shoulder. He pulled out his gold snuffbox and gave himself a healthy smack.

The auction block was already open since midmorning. We latecomers were added to the sweltering nonhuman cargo. We slaves came in all colors, genders, ages, and abilities. Ours was a pariah market. You could think of us as vegetables, cattle, fish, or fowl or anything but human beings with immortal souls. Owners thought of us as another table or chair, something to be used and disposed of when, through no fault of its own, it has become useless.

The auctioneer, a large man, six feet tall with long black hair hanging from underneath his dark-green three-corner hat, stood wilting in the hot sun and sweltering humidity. He wore a soiled light-blue-green wilted suit. He reined in back at the auctioneer's podium. His right arm was raised. His right hand was holding a large wooden gavel. Six slaves—four men and two women—on the selling platform crowded together, sweated together, and supported one another from falling off the platform.

The bidding began. The auctioneer slammed his gavel again and again for attention. The buyers' attention turned to inspect the items for sale.

"What am I bidding for this fine, strong buck?" called the auctioneer.

"One peso!" Someone howled.

"This stallion will produce great future stallions for your plantation. I can't let him go for less than twenty pesos," argued the auctioneer.

"Eight pesos!" cried another buyer.

"Eight would be a steal. Fifteen would be a giveaway," winced the auctioneer, waving his gavel above his head.

"Ten!" bellowed another deep voice from the back of the crowd of buyers.

"Twelve!" screeched a high-pitched utterance.

"Fifteen!" demanded a determined whisperer.

All eyes glared at the strong-willed bidder. They felt his two-balled pertinacity in the pit of their stomachs. His fearsome whisper cowed their intent to outbid such a notorious scoundrel. Their silence forced the auctioneer to raise his gavel and proclaim, "Fifteen pesos!" Banging his gavel, he continued, "Going once. Going twice. And going three times. Sold!"

The winner stood up. With a dash of his right hand, he wiped the perspiration off his forehead. His eyes narrowed into tight slits. His mouth pursed and spit out a wad of chewing tobacco. He wiped his lips with a white lacy handkerchief. His purple silk suit with its white-colored lace ran with sweat. The long curly black hairs that protruded from his ears and nostrils dripped with sweat. With a twist of his right hand, he commanded his slave master to pick up his new property with a whispered warning: "Do not damage an inch of that magnificent torso."

Finally, all the other slaves had been auctioned off. Now it was our turn to stand on the auction platform. I held Catalina's hand to steady her. Grast held Safira's hand to calm her anxious resentment about this whole situation. Corte stood tall. With his scarred head held high, he looked like El Cid.

"Behold, our fine selection of genuine Gypsy slaves," boasted the auctioneer. "One strong man and his fertile wife, and two young studs still wet behind their ears. The woman will read your future in tea leaves and the palm of your hand. And the stallions will work their asses off for your plantation needs. The noble-looking, scar-faced gentleman has a limp leg, but he can wash dishes and scrub floors like a cat catching a canary." He paused. He cleared his throat loudly. "Now, you can buy them as a group or as singles. Eighty pesos for the group." He twirled his gavel in the air. "Or as singles, twenty pesos each." He eyed the crowd eagerly for a first bid.

The air rustled with anxious voices outabducting one another with variations of *ohs* and *ahs*.

"Forty for the whole herd," yelled a surreptitious old codger with a sneaky wink in his left eye.

"Ten for the mare," bolted a villainous gent with a long black twirled-up mustache.

"Fifty for the whole herd," voiced a powerful man with huge hands and massive body parts.

"Twelve for the old stallion," intoned the voice of a squirrely senor in a huge sombrero.

"Sixty for the whole passel," concluded a dapper old fogy with a large gold ring in his left earlobe.

Before the auctioneer could bang his gavel for peace, a man dressed in a dark-blue cape and hood bid, "Eighty for the five."

A hush fell over the crowd. The auctioneer stared in disbelief.

"Eighty pesos for the five human beings," repeated the man in the cloak.

"Eighty-two," piped a teaser.

"Ninety pesos for all," offered the man in the dark-blue cloak.

A loud hush fell over the crowd.

The auctioneer stared in disbelief. "Going once. Going twice. Going three times. Sold!"

The man in the cloak beckoned us to come to him with his white right hand.

We stood before him in silence.

He spoke. "You are free. You can go your way, or you can come to work for me. I will pay a just salary."

We had no money. We had no place to go to stay. We accepted.

"Yes," I said.

"Yes," echoed Grast, Safira, Catalina, and Corte.

"Well then, welcome to New Spain. My name is Padre Antonio. We will travel to the Valle del Rio Pajaro in California. You can help build a new mission there. You can work and become a part of our mission congregation."

"How far is this new mission?" I asked.

"About three or four weeks walking."

"A breeze," exhaled Grast.

"Your salary begins today," said the Padre.

"Great balls of fire! Let's go!" chimed Safira for the rest of us.

Corte nodded.

CHAPTER 8

New Spain cried out, "Adventure."

Promises abounded.

Aztecs shriveled in astonishment.

Spaniards craved for gold.

Padre Antonio led us from Port San Sabastiano to Cholula, to Tlaxcala, to Tecoacino, and to many more small villages on our way to Tenochtitlan, the Aztec name for Mexico City. It was like walking through a wonderland of the remnants of a once proud and powerful people who had been devastated by an unimaginable foe from the sea. A foe with strange things that they had never seen before. They had never seen a horse. They had never seen things made of steel: a steel helmet and armor, a steel sword, a steel gun, or a cannon that projected metal objects that killed people and demolished walls and buildings. All these things were supernatural for them, a dream from the depths of a blazing cauldron of darkness like an earthquake.

From the time of Hernando Cortez, in the early 1500s, to our time, the late 1700s, these native people suffered under the Spanish heel.

The once proud pyramids of polished stones, dedicated to their many gods, like Xiuhtecuhtli, the fire lord, stood shamefully like naked giants stripped off their golden trappings, a pile of broken bones and smashed teeth. Small scantily clad children with their sticks and handballs ran up and down those broken steps, playing their games of ancient origin.

Padre Antonio smiled at the little children and quoted Holy Scripture to us. "Blessed are the poor, for they shall inherit the earth."

"How is that possible, Padre?" asked Grast.

"Well, the poor native families have many, many, many children, while the rich Spanish families produce only one or two or no children. Eventually, the rich will fade away and the poor will take over the earth."

"Very good!" replied Grast. "Maybe there's hope for us poor Gypsy families too. We say that the earth is our home and the sky is our roof."

Finally, we arrived at the hilltop that gave us a view of Montezuma's capital, Tenochtitlan, now called Mexico City. Its canals' once azure-blue and clean, sparkling waters are now muddy and trashy. They reminded me of a picture that I'd seen in school, a picture of Venice, Italy.

Padre Antonio pointed out the prominent buildings, the remains of temple ruins once the pride of gods like

Quetzalcoatl, the snake god. Now, crosses topped these shattered temple-pyramids. Their gold and jeweled artifacts had long been sacked and melted down. They became prizes for the king and queen of Spain and their nobles.

The padre pointed out the palace of Montezuma and his father, Axayacatl. It was now the seat of the Spanish government.

A mist, like the web of a giant black widow spider, covered the entire city. In the center of the web sat the giant spider. Her belly was decorated with the red-and-yellow flag of Spain. Her fangs sucked gold and silver for her king and countrymen.

Padre Antonio told us, "I'm going to visit our obispo and ask for the needs of our new Mission de Santa Lucia, in the Valle del Rio Pajaro. Why don't you go visit the shrine of the Black Virgin, Our Lady of Guadalupe, at Tepeyac Hill. She appeared there to the young Aztec man Juan Diego on December 9, 10, and 12, 1531. The Aztecs call her Tecoatlaxope, meaning "she will crush the serpent of stone Quetzalcoatl."

"What is there to see?" asked Safira.

"Why, the tilma, or cloak, of Juan Diego. That's where the image of Our Lady appeared. She is wearing the garments of an Aztec princess," replied the padre.

"Oh, I want to feel that," cried Cato.

"Me too," I added as Cato and I were still wearing our masculine disguises.

"Go ahead," encouraged the padre. "Pray that the obispo will give the material needs that will help build up our new mission."

"You go, and we'll pray," chimed Safira and Grast.

Corte nodded.

As we approached the small shrine on Tepeyac Hill, we saw and smelled the pink cloud of the roses of Castile. They reminded me of the beautiful and fragrant roses of my father's garden at home near Cádiz, Spain.

Cato could smell the sweet, warm perfume, like the intoxicating aroma of honeysuckle at midnight. She took a deep breath of the heavenly sweet fragrance and asked, "Would it be all right for me, a Jew, to enter this shrine?"

I looked at her and teased, "It would be wrong if you did not go in, Cato. Everyone with love in their hearts is welcome. Our Lady loves you just as much as she loves all her Aztec children."

As we approached the small wooden shrine, we noticed the Aztec pilgrims walking on their knees, with their rosary beads in their hands. I guided Catalina around them.

Inside the chapel-shrine, the dim yellow light of many candles helped us to see the tilma of Juan Diego with the image of Our Lady on it hanging next to the crucifix on the wall in back of the altar. A large brace of candles lit up the tilma so that we could see the smoke-stained image of Our Lady. The blue green of her cape and the pink of her dress complimented her glowing face that looked lovingly at each one of us.

I asked Catalina, "Would you like to stand or kneel as there are no seats?"

"I'll kneel," she replied. "I feel a deep sense of prayer here."

We walked on our knees with the rest of the pilgrims until we reached the image of Our Lady. Then our hands reached out to touch the hem of the tilma. I held Catalina's hand to touch the holy cloth. She smiled. Her face glowed with an inner light. I was stunned. She relaxed.

"What happened?" I asked.

"I saw her marvelous face in my mind's eye. Her eyes contained the reflected images of Juan Diego. She spoke to me. She told me, 'You will see all things with the eyes of your heart.'"

I paused. I did not want to disturb her sense of peace. I prayed a Hail Mary in silence as tears began to roll down my cheeks. Then we arose to give our place to other pilgrims.

Once outside, we rested on the smooth rocks near the pink roses of Castile. Catalina picked a blossom and placed it next to her heart. I remembered her saying she will see all things with the eyes of her heart.

Padre Antonio walked up Tepeyac Hill, leading two mules loaded with supplies. "How goes it, pilgrims?" He smiled, waving his free hand. "Meet Rosie and Rufus." The mules brayed, displaying their long yellowish teeth. "We got almost half of what I asked for."

"Well, as we Gypsies say, 'Half a loaf is better than nothing,'" boasted Grast. "When do we proceed to the mission?"

"We can start now and reach the first of our mission stops by evening. I have some finger food for our lunch. We can stop under the first oak tree and eat."

Safira held up her hand and said, "Wait a minute! Padre, could we take some slips from these roses of Castile for the new mission? They would remind us of our visit to this shrine and Our Lady of Guadalupe."

"By all means, take as many as you wish. But wrap them in some wet sacking lest they die before we reach the Valle del Pajaro," warned Padre Antonio.

"Yes, Padre," replied Safira.

"Remember," continued the padre, "these are the roses that bloomed in the winter, out of season, when Our Lady told Juan Diego to fill his tilma with them and bring them to the obispo to prove that her message to build a shrine here at Tepeyac was the truth."

"And did the obispo believe?" I asked.

"Jaco, the obispo saw the roses fall to the floor. He smiled condescendingly. But when he saw the image of Our Lady on Juan's tilma, his eyes bulged in disbelief. Then he knelt and believed."

"We'll need at least a dozen slips for the new mission garden," whispered Cato. "I'll always remember their sweet fragrance."

"Here, Safira," nodded Grast. "Take my knife. Cut at least twelve slips for the new mission, and take twelve more, just in case some do not survive the trip."

Corte, like a shadow of hope, leaned forward. His scared hands held the rose stems.

I, Jacaranda, wrapped the souvenir clippings in dampened sackcloth. Then I placed the package on Rosie's back.

"Well, Corte," grinned Grast, "we can be mule skinners for our glorious adventure to the Valle del Pajaro."

As Corte smiled, some of the scars on his face reassembled, like the pieces of a jigsaw puzzle.

I studied that puzzled face. I thought that I saw pieces that I had seen somewhere. But I could not put them together in my memory.

Padre Antonio tightened the wide black belt on his dark-blue habit. "Look yonder, see that black oak on the top of that first hill. That'll be our first stop for lunch."

"Hallelujah!" yelled Safira. "I'm starved."

"The hand food isn't much, but it should hold us until we reach the first mission for dinner and a good night's sleep," offered Padre Antonio.

We embraced one another as a sign of peace. Then we began our hiking with the mules' pace. I thanked God, who gave mules a pace that would not wear them or us out.

After lunch, we left the shade of the old oak tree. Padre Antonio guided us through some of the most beautiful country that I've ever seen. It was spring. Some fields were covered in a waving display of bright-yellow mustard plant blossoms. As we passed through the welcome shade of an oak forest, I could see patches of golden-yellow poppies. The next hillside would be a spread of bright-blue lupine.

A yellow meadowlark darted out from the grass in front of me. I jumped. There were other surprises. Squirrels, chipmunks, raccoons, deer, and black bears were all curious about the strangers visiting parts of their forest.

The natural beauty of this land was a breath of fresh air after prisons, pirates, and slavery.

CHAPTER 9

Poppies nodded heads of gold.

Spaniards craved for gold.

Spain's king sold California for gold

Natives lost all rights.

P adre Antonio led us, day by day, from one mission to the next. There we spent the night. We ate. We prayed. We slept.

"Jaco and Cato," whispered Grast. "Keep wearing your masculine disguises. They will protect you from the soldiers at the fort near each mission."

"Yes," added Safira. "Some of them look like they haven't seen a woman for months."

"We'll look tough and grumble about most things," sighed Catalina, tossing her head from side to side. She adjusted her eye patches. "That's how the sailors and pirates acted."

"Yes," I continued. "My brother, Christabo, was a champion at that."

"Stick close to Grast and me," advised Corte. "Our eye patches will help show them how tough we are."

"Oh yes," muttered Grast. "You might moisten your neck charm. Its stink will send suitors skedaddling."

So far we have passed through the native land of the Diegueños, the Luiseños, the Serranos, and the Chumashes. All these people looked healthy and strong. They earned their living by hunting wild game like deer, antelope, rabbits, and moose; by gathering berries, seeds, and acorns; by fishing; by catching abalone; and by digging for clams.

Most of these natives wore no clothing. They reminded me of what God intended us to look like in his Garden of Eden.

The spring weather was mild. Rain came in short and sweet refreshments.

Children, like fawns and bear cubs, played and ran together. I envied their openheartedness. Their cultural habit of living naturally as God made them continued into their adulthood. The men adorned their heads with tule caps decorated with feathers or seashells as a form of personal identity. The rest of their body was to be admired as a gift from God. Later, they might embellish their torso with animal hides and strings of seashell beads or acorns to signify a feast day or social standing in the tribe. On cold days, a daub of mud kept the torso warm.

Women wore facial tattoos for tribal recognition. Short lap skirts of tule or hides were the fashion. On cool days, they might don a robe of deer hide or otter pelts or a grizzly bear fur. Some liked to wear strands of seashell beads or acorns around their necks. Some wove flowers or seashells into their long black hair, like sunshine sparkling on the sea.

The coastal area was free from snow and ice. I learned that snow could be seen in the winter on the top of the mountains to the east. The ocean gave gentle breezes of clean, refreshing air.

I wondered how many people from Spain would love to come here. Here where there were no garbage-filled streets, no winter snows to shovel, no flooding rains with hail and ice. They could bask in the coastal California sunshine and enjoy fiestas and bear fights and bullfights.

How long would it take them to recreate in California the same dirty, overcrowded city that they had left in Spain?

"Oh, Padre, I just love this California coastal area. It's so naturally beautiful. And the natives blend in so well with its Garden of Eden atmosphere."

"Yes," Padre Antonio added. "Our King of Spain has given us the work of saving California for Spain. He's afraid that Russia will send down colonizers from Alaska to settle and claim California for Russia."

"Where are the Russians now?" I asked.

"They have a settlement down as far as Fort Ross, just miles north of the San Francisco Bay Area. Our king wants our missions to begin settlements as far as both sides of the San Francisco Bay Area."

"Well, so far, you've only reached this Monterey Bay area. How soon can you settle all the sides of the San Francisco Bay Area?"

"Were going as fast as we can," replied the padre.

"Your mission in the Valle del Rio Pajaro is one small step in the right direction," I added.

"Yes, Jaco, and we hope to achieve the final goal soon." The padre touched his nose with his right index finger and shook his head in a negative way. He took a deep breath and continued, "We have to be very careful. The first group of missionaries who came before us settled their missions in Lower California." He clutched his right hand into a fist and shoved it high toward the sun. Then he clenched his mouth and lips into a sharp line of pain and frustration.

"We have to be very careful. Those missionaries were too successful. They trained the natives to develop huge rancheros around each mission. They developed huge herds of cattle and horses. The cow hides stacked up and were sold to ships for good piles of pesos. The natives learned to raise grapes and produce wine. They learned to tan leather. They learned to make candles from the fat of the cattle. Their gardens produced beautiful crops of fruits and vegetables.

"The goal was to turn the rancheros over to the natives. They, in turn, would become the new citizens of New Spain.

"But our jealous Spanish pioneers, failing to find fortunes, coveted the riches of those rancheros for themselves. They spread lies about the padres. They accused them of treason to our king. The Spanish king, together with the kings of France and Portugal and other European countries, challenged the pope to disband the Jesuits. In 1773, Pope Clement XIV issued a Brief of Suppression to extinguish the Jesuits.

"The missionaries found no refuge in all Europe or the New World. However, Catherine the Great of Russia, a former Lutheran turned Russian Orthodox Christian, welcomed them to accept her hospitality in Russia. They continued to teach in her college at St. Petersburg." The padre smiled his broadest grin and nodded toward Russian Alaska and Fort Ross. "The greedy Spaniards seized the rancheros and made the natives their slaves." The padre bit his lip and added, "Then the king of Spain ordered our Sociedad de la Estrella del Mar in our dark-blue habits to develop new missions in Upper California."

"Would the same thing happen again if you become too successful?" I asked.

"It could." Padre Antonio crossed himself and silently prayed that it would not happen.

"Let's pray that it doesn't," chimed Cato. "Let's pray that greed doesn't destroy our good padres' work to help the natives to learn the Spanish language and Spanish ways. They could run their own rancheros for themselves and their children."

"The king of Spain made ugly laws against us Gypsies too," grinned Grast, shaking his head and baring his missing-teeth smile. "He exempted us from the Privilege of Sanctuary. The police could drag us out of any church and kill us." He spat on the ground. "Are the natives learning Spanish and Spanish ways?"

"It's a hard task," pondered Padre Antonio. "They live so comfortably in their ways. Our ways of dressing and living together often confuse them."

Grast looked confused and said, "Should they become like us, or should we become like them?"

"That's a good question, Grast," answered the padre.

"Maybe," I added, "we should learn from one another."

Safira prayed, "Yes! Let's hope that greed doesn't ruin the good work of our padres."

"The king of Spain made laws against my people, the Jews, and the Moors too. He made it legal to seize our property and kill us if we did not become Catholics," pined Cato.

"Our king did not understand people." Corte winced. "Some of the ranchero owners did. They invited Gypsies to live safely on their rancheros."

"That's what saved Grast and me," said Safira. "Our owner had his faults, but he was a real human being too."

Corte's twisted face tried to smile.

I looked at his good right eye. I thought that I saw something that I'd seen before, but I could not remember what or when.

"We should arrive at the mission for the Esselen people by evening," announced our padre. "Then we should reach our home mission, Mission Santa Lucia, in the Valle del Pajaro by tomorrow evening. Then you will meet our Calendaruc people."

"Hooray!" yelled Safira. "I've never walked so far. My feet are killing me."

CHAPTER 10

Native Californians

Sang their final song,

Dancing on the brink of the world,

Shouting to the sun.

The sky was alive with bird sounds. Clouds upon clouds of gulls, cormorants, geese, ducks, herons, curlews, sandpipers, and dowitchers smothered the heavens with feathers, feet, and bills of every size and color. Like characters in a Chinese poem, each bird never missed its meter. The muted flapping of wings, the constant chatter of the highs and lows of different bird tongues composed a Rio del Pajaro symphony. Birds owned the sky.

I looked at Cato. She smiled. She waved her arms. She conducted the music of the birds.

"Imagine," I said to Cato, Grast, Safira, Corte, and Padre Antonio, "thousands of flying birds without one bird crashing into another."

"Yes," answered Grast. "Horses could learn a lot from them."

"Yes," added Corte. "We could all learn to get along together better from these birds."

"Each bird knows his or her own flight pattern in their own bird cloud. They respect one another's space," said Padre Antonio.

"Each cloud of birds," exclaimed Safira, "flies without disturbing the clouds of birds surrounding them."

"Yes," mused Padre Antonio. "Nations could learn a lot from those fair and stormy clouds of feathered friends."

"Here's where we cross the Rio del Pajaro," announced Padre Antonio. He stooped to remove his sandals and his blue habit. Then he rolled them together in a bundle. "Strip down to your bare necessities. You can hold your bundle of clothes high over your head as we ford the *rio*. Follow me carefully. I know where all the rocks are."

Cato asked me quietly, "How much do we take off? I hope our walnut stain is waterproof."

I replied, "Keep enough on to maintain our disguise. I'll hold your hand to guide you through the water."

"*Burr!*" yelled Safira. "This water is cold." She held her bundle high. Deft footwork helped her to follow the padre from rock to rock.

Corte followed Safira. His one good eye caught sight of the abundant salmon population.

Grast came next. He stooped from the first rock to grab a large crawdad. With his mouth of alternating, missing teeth, he chomped the critter, sweet meat, shell and all.

I led Cato, rock by rock, to the other shore.

On the north bank of the river, we dressed. Before us lay a forest of redwood trees. Under the low branches of one redwood tree stood some naked natives. The look on the oldest man's face questioned why we were bothering to cover up our God-given bodies with those old rags. His eyes shared the idea that they could cross the river without taking anything on or off. He seemed to be thinking, *When will these foreigners learn to be as practical as us Calendaruc people?*

I hope that I haven't read too much into that man's facial expression. It's just that his eyebrows kept going up and down with an arched curve of exasperation.

"I see that some of our Calendaruc people are here to greet us," said Padre Antonio. "They only wear their mission clothes when they go to the mission."

"Will we be expected to undress like them when we go to their village?" asked Safira.

"No," answered the padre. "But it's at times like this river crossing that I admire their practicality."

"Padre?" I asked. "I noticed how white your skin is."

"Yes," he replied. "I'm an albino."

Grast heard us. He walked over to us and looked into the padre's eyes. "Your eyes are pink."

"Yes," Padre replied. "All albinos' eyes are pink."

"I remember seeing an albino boy on our ranchero near Cádiz. He used to come and ask for food. We never knew where he came from or where he was going. Then one day, he just disappeared. We never saw him again."

"That could have been me," the padre said while adjusting the blue hood of his habit over his white hair.

Safira listened to us. She remembered my baptismal celebration. "I remember an albino boy," she said. "He came to our ranchero on Jacaranda's baptismal day celebration. We gave him food. Then Christabo, Jacaranda's older brother, took him for a walk behind the barn. When Christabo returned, he hid his hands. When I went into the chapel, I saw blood on the baptismal font."

"That sounds right," said the padre. "The boy beat me. I bled. He gave all the food to the pigs. I ran."

"We never knew that," said Grast.

"I'm so sorry," said Safira.

Corte listened and hung his head.

I bit my lip. *How could my brother have been so mean? He was mean to his horse, but this boy was bringing food to hungry people.*

I guided Cato to the mission. The trail led us through a beautiful forest of redwood trees. The trees came in all sizes. The giants were in the two-hundred-foot range. The rest varied from infant to child, to teenage, to adult. The sunlight filtering through the broad branches and dark-green leaves cast lacelike shadows on our hands and faces.

This Valle del Rio Pajaro was a place of nature's peaceful magic. I glanced at a small glen of green grass. I saw a mother deer with her two fauns nibbling the grass. The mother looked up at us. Her eyes invited us to nibble with them.

Padre Antonio led us to a large meadow with a sparkling stream of water running through it.

"Here is the site for our new Mission Santa Lucia," he said, pointing to a row of tule reed huts.

"At home at last!" exclaimed Safira.

"Yes," added Padre Antonio. "The young man in his mission clothing is Silver Fox. He is the son of Gray Wolf, the tribal leader of the Calendaruc people."

"Has he learned Spanish?" I asked.

"Yes. He's a quick learner."

"Has he been baptized?"

"No, he still has some questions." Padre Antonio closed his eyes tightly. "Someday, God's grace will help him to believe."

Padre Antonio turned away from me and addressed Silver Fox. "Greetings, meet our new friends from Spain. The man with the scarred face and a patch over his left eye is Corte. The man with the withered left hand is Grast. The lady with the sparkling eyes is Safira. The young man with patches over both eyes is Cato. And the young man with the patch over his right eye is Jaco. They have all come to help us build our new Mission Santa Lucia. Friends, meet Silver Fox."

We all took turns saying hellos and shaking hands with Silver Fox. I liked his smile. It revealed a row of strong white teeth. His eyes were a deep, dark brown. A certain warmth flowed from them. When he looked at me and Cato, there was a certain question mark on his forehead.

Padre Antonio continued speaking to Silver Fox, "They will need a new family hut. Can you show them how to find and cut willow branches to frame their hut and to find tule to make bundles and mats to cover the frame and floor?"

"Yes, I will be pleased to help." Silver Fox nodded.

Grast hesitated, then he spoke, "Maybe we should have three smaller huts. Safira and I should be alone. Corte needs privacy. And Cato and Jaco are good friends."

"Yes," agreed Padre Antonio. "That sounds reasonable."

"All of you can follow Silver Fox and help cut and carry the tule and willow branches," said the padre. He took his rosary beads and said, "I'm going to the chapel hut and pray."

"Wait a minute," interrupted Safira. "I want to plant the rose of Castile cuttings before they die. I'll need Cato to help. Padre, please show us where you want your mission garden to be."

"Right over there." Padre Antonio pointed to a sunny glen. "That's where the adobe mission will stand. Plant in the space to the right and the left of the markers for the front door."

"Thank you, Padre," chimed Safira and Cato. They left to find Rosie the mule and the rose clippings.

Silver Fox and his native helpers taught us how to cut and assemble the material. We finished our new homes in time for dinner. By this time, we were used to strange foods like acorn soup, deliciously rich and oily acorn bread, mouthwatering abalone, and enjoyable gophers or quail. For appetizers, there could be grasshoppers, yellow jacket grubs, or a fat lizard or snake. Only a few animals were taboo for religious reasons: eagles, buzzards, ravens, owls, and frogs. These people were not agricultural. They had no need to plant food. It grew naturally in the ocean, in the streams and rivers, in the sloughs and marshlands, in the forest trees and bushes. The wild birds' eggs were there for the picking. They could hunt for birds and animals in season. The men were serious hunters. Before going to hunt, the men refrained from sex and food. They spent days in the sweathouse to rid themselves of their human smell to be able to sneak up on their prey unnoticed.

After dinner, Padre Antonio asked, "Would you like to have Silver Fox show you the history of his people on the slab of an old redwood tree?"

"Oh yes," Cato replied. "I'm fascinated by new cultures. I want to know as much as I can about them."

"Do they know where their ancestors came from?" asked Grast. "We Gypsies only have a vague idea where our ancestors came from. Somewhere in India through Egypt is our best guess. Nobody bothered to write it down for us to remember."

"Here is the crosscut round slab of the old redwood tree," said Padre Antonio. "It fell last year. So we know that the last outer ring must be for our last year, 1775. There are over three thousand rings on this tree. So it must have been growing here one thousand, almost two thousand years before the birth of Jesus Christ."

"Amazing!" cried Corte. "Some of these trees here are twice as big around as this tree. Imagine how old they must be."

"There is something sacred about this grove of trees," sighed Safira. "I feel a divine presence."

"My eighteen years of life is almost nothing compared to these trees," cried Cato.

"Yes, Cato, I agree," I whispered.

"Yes," continued Padre Antonio. "We are privileged to see this natural beauty of California before our Spanish countrymen come to cut and sell these trees for gold.

"The Calendaruc people have never touched these living trees. They only harvest branches and bark from the fallen trees." He paused and turned to Silver Fox. "Now it is Silver Fox's turn to tell about his people."

"Thank you, Padre," said Silver Fox. "Coyote and Eagle created our world before this tree was born. Then they created all the plants and trees as living signs of their love for us. At last they created all the animals, birds, and beasts, large and small, for us. Finally, they created us and put us in this beautiful garden. They told us what to eat and not to eat. They told us how to hunt and gather our food. A successful hunter is called *koxoenis*—a bringer of meat."

"When did your people come to this Valle del Pajaro?" asked Corte.

"We believe that our tribes came from the north. But we are forbidden to speak of the dead or to mention their names or to recall their deeds."

"Yes," interrupted Padre Antonio. "That's why it is so hard to find a history of these people. However, we have found shell mounds in this area that indicate that these people have been here for four thousand to five thousand years."

"That would put them back to when this great tree was just a sapling," added Grast.

"Yes," replied Padre Antonio. "We can thank them for keeping this valley so beautiful."

"Their generations have kept these trees and the rivers and streams in their natural condition. Just wait till the Spaniards settle here. Good by natural conditions," sighed Safira.

"Jesus was born in the year 1 according to our calendar. That would put him about halfway to the center of this slab," I estimated.

"Yes," added Cato. "And the time of Abraham and his sons, Isaac and Ishmael, would be about halfway between Jesus and the center of this tree."

"And," added Padre Antonio, "Silver Fox's people were already well along with their many shell mounds."

"Thank you, Silver Fox, for your sharing. I want to know more about your people," I said.

"So do I," said Cato.

"Look at the stars!" I exclaimed.

"Yes," answered Padre Antonio. "They are so big and bright here. That's why I want to call this mission after them in honor of Our Lady "Star of the Sea," Estrella del Mar. We call the mountain at the back of this valley in her honor too, Monte Madonna."

"You would have named this valley after her," said Silver Fox, "if we had not already called it after our patron, the Eagle, the Valle del Rio Pajaro."

"Yes, Silver Fox," answered Padre. "You beat us to the punch."

"Well," replied Padre Antonio, "it's time to retire. May God bless you all. Good night."

We all agreed and walked to our huts.

"How's this for a fine new home?" I asked Cato.

Cato reclined on the tule-mat floor. She covered herself with one of the otter robes that Silver Fox had given to us.

"Now we can sleep without the snores and gas explosions of our fellow man." She smoothed her hand over the otter fur. Cato smiled and slept.

Suddenly, a loud clanging sound shattered our silence. Horns screamed. A deep man's voice yelled, "Everybody up!"

I jumped up and looked out of our hut. I saw lighted torches passing through the forest. Men on horses and foot came roughshod through the meadow toward the mission huts.

Padre Antonio came out of his hut. He waved his arms over his head and cried, "What's all this noise about? Who are you?"

The captain ran his horse up close to the padre and pulled on the reins. His horse stood on his hind legs and clawed the air with his front legs. Then his front hooves came down in front of Padre Antonio. Dust covered the padre's blue habit, but the padre stood firm. He said, "Who are you? What is the meaning of all this nonsense?"

The captain tipped his helmet and shook its white-plumed topknot at the padre. "This is an arrest."

"For what and whom?" replied the padre.

"For heretics!" snapped the captain.

"You must be crazy. We have no heretics here."

"Oh yes, you have." The captain spit. "They came from the slaver galleon from Cádiz."

"There were only pirates and slaves on that galleon. I know. I bought five slaves and set them free."

"You bought five heretics." The captain spit again and smiled. "You could be burned at the stake for helping heretics. Where are they? Turn them in right now and avoid the fire!"

We five stood in front of our huts. We looked at one another. Our faces agreed to save the padre. "Here we are!" yelled Grast.

We nodded a yes and waved our hands high over our heads. My eyes watered.

"See there, Padre. There are your heretics. They saved your neck by volunteering."

"You should not have done that," our padre whispered to us. "I'll save you."

"Like hell you will!" shouted the captain. "Tie that padre up with the rest of them."

The soldiers lost no time in trussing us up with ropes and manacles. There were four foot soldiers to guard each one of us. I was the first one behind the captain and his men on their horses. The rest followed on foot.

"All right, men," ordered the captain. "Let us proceed to the Presidio in Monterey."

We marched. The torches carried by the men on horseback lighted our way. It was a very dark night. The fog became dense. The grizzly bears growled. The wolves howled. When we reached the Monterey area, we heard the sea lions arguing among themselves. When we entered the presidio, I turned to look at my fellow captives. There were none there.

The captain saluted the guards at the presidio gate. Then he turned to look at his captives. I was the only one remaining. "Place that captive"—he pointed at me—"in the safest prison cell. Then report to me."

I wondered what had happened to the rest of my friends.

CHAPTER 11

Calendarucs, God's people,

Harvested God's crops.

Spaniards demolished God's plans for peace.

Who survived to tell?

The presidio's prison cells were not built by Gypsies. I could not move the window bars like the ones in Cádiz. No Grast was here to save me. I lay down on a straw-filled mattress and tried to sleep.

"Wake up!" a low, dark voice whispered.

I woke up. My eyes stared into the darkness of my cell. "Who's there?" I whispered, hoping to hear a friend.

"I'm a friend. I have a key. How friendly can you be?"

"I'm open to any friend. Come in."

"Thanks." A key clicked in the lock.

The door opened. A face that I'd never seen before stared at me through the moonlight from the cell window. I saw a broken nose between two deep-set dark eyes. A lugubrious mouth dripped saliva from its swollen lower lip's corners. He stepped into the cell and walked toward me. He knelt next to me. His hands cupped my face.

I shuddered at his touch. "What's your name?"

"Jose. What's yours?"

"Jaco."

"Well, Jaco, I like your soft skin."

"How can you help me?"

"I've come to free you, if you do right by me." He released his hands from my face and slid them down the sides of my arms. He ended by pinching my rear end.

"Wait a minute!" I yelled. "I'm not your patsy. Get off me. Now!"

"Just a minute, I'll get to the best part fast." Both hands reach to my crotch. "What the hell!" he shouted. "You're no Jaco. You're a Jaca!" He tore my shirt to reveal my breasts. "Well, this might be better than I thought."

I fought. My fists hit his wet lips and sunken eyes. I pushed against his chest and arms. I shouted, "Stop! Stop! Help! Help!" I yelled as loudly as I could. I hoped that someone would hear me and come to my aid. He was too big for me to stop his madness. I could only continue to scream. "Help! Someone, please help!"

"What's all the fuss?" another dark voice called out in the darkness.

"This man's trying to rape me!"

"Oh ho!" called the stranger. "Up to your old tricks, Jose!"

"None of your business!" yelled Jose!

"Oh yes, it is!" responded the stranger. "Get up and get out of here. I'll have you horsewhipped till the skin falls off your bony back."

Jose jumped up. He bolted out the door.

I breathed a sigh of relief.

"Are you hurt?" the stranger asked.

"I'm shaken but all right." I asked, "Who are you?"

"I'm Padre Franco Gonzalez, the presidio chaplain. Jose has a bad habit of molesting young men prisoners. I'll report him to the captain. He'll get his whipping."

"Thank you, Padre Franco. I appreciate your help. Padre Antonio has been a good friend."

"Yes, I know him well. We are good friends. I saw you when you came in tonight. I saw through your disguise."

"We, my friend Catalina and I, are disguised as Gypsy men. Our friend Grast, a Gypsy, thought it would be wise to protect us from the men on our trip."

"That was good," agreed the padre. "However, a relative of yours is here to bring you to justice, Padre Fernando Salmanez and his helper, Friar Pablo."

I paused. *Not again*, I thought to myself. "What does he want?" I asked.

"He issued the order to have you all arrested as heretics."

"It all starts over again," I said. "The Inquisition never lets go."

"No," added Padre Franco. "It hangs on like a mad dog. Your friends were rescued last night by the natives. Silver Fox arranged a hunting party to shoot the soldiers with poison darts. Then they led your friends to a cave on Monte Madonna. They left you and your guards alone. Your group was just behind the captain. He might have noticed your disappearance. They buried the soldiers in places where they will never be found. He got word to me. He wanted me to help you to escape. I have a fast horse ready to take you to the rock caves by the ocean. You will be safe there until Silver Fox rescues you."

"How will I find the caves in the dark?" I asked.

"Just listen for the sea lions. Their barking will lead you to them."

"Anything in a storm," I always say.

"Now, follow me."

I followed the padre into the dark night. We came to the presidio stables. There he saddled a fine black stallion. I patted his mane and spoke into his ear like I used to do to Eclipse. He whinnied and nuzzled my ear. I knew that we were friends.

"What is the name of this horse?" I asked.

"Fluss," Padre Franco replied. "It's an Arabic name for an Arabian horse. It means 'money.'"

"How clever," I answered. "How expensive was he?"

"Plenty."

"Well, I must be off. Wish me luck."

"Follow the sound of the sea lions. Fluss will do the rest. Adios."

"Thank you for all the help. May God bless you."

"And you too." I gave Fluss a hug and whispered in his ear, "Let's go, big boy."

Fluss knew his business. He brought me to places where the sound of the sea lions grew louder and louder. It began to rain. Lightning flashed and revealed the rocky cliff above the ocean far below. *I must be near the caves where I'm supposed to hide.* I dismounted.

"Fluss, you've done your job well. Now, go home." I patted his rump, and away he trotted.

In the purple night, I stood alone. *By God, I'll do this if it kills me.* Lightning flashed again. I covered my eyes with my lower arms clasped together. *I must not be afraid.* My clothes were all wet. Somewhere, I had lost my shoes.

The rain came down in torrents. I balanced myself on my bare feet, standing on a high, rocky cliff above the Pacific Ocean. Strong winds and heavy rain fought to unsteady my body. Several times I almost fell. But I regained my balance again and again.

Without moon and starlight, I really could not see where I was going. Only by feel, my hands groped from one wet rock to another. I thought of Catalina without her eyes. *Only the eyes of her heart could show her the way. May the eyes of my heart help me now.*

I listened to the crashing of the waves on the rocks far below. *Do not be afraid*, I kept repeating to myself over and over again.

In the distant dark blur of the stormy night, I saw flickering lights. They grew larger each minute. *Could they be the torches of a search party from the presidio? Has Padre Fernando organized a search party to take me back for another trial, to be burned alive as a witch?*

I fumbled. I grabbed rock after rock to lower myself down to find a cave to hide in. My hands and feet began to bleed. The eyes of my heart searched for a cave. Every time I hoped to see one, my hands felt hard rock. Suddenly, my head began to whirl. Lightning flashed. The rain beat down on me. I fell. Down, down, down, my body entered the splashing surf. The cold, cold, cold water numbed every inch of my body. I struggled with every inch of energy left in my body. My arms flayed the water. They searched for something to grab, a rock, a piece of driftwood, anything.

Suddenly, a strong warm hand clasped my small cold wrist. It pulled me up, out of the water. I was hanging in midair above the waves. I could not scream. Deep in my heart I prayed for God's mercy. I felt myself being lowered down as the sound of crashing waves grew louder and louder in my ears.

Suddenly, my feet felt the softness of something pliable, a tule mat. The touch and its swaying motion suggested a raft or a canoe. The strong hand lowered me to rest on this floating refuge.

"Stay still," whispered a soft, deep masculine voice.

"Yes," I responded. "But who are you?"

"Be still. Rest."

I closed my eyes. My ears heard the sound of a paddle slapping against rocks. Then the paddle churned against treacherous waters. The unrelenting wind blew spindrift off the waves. The salty foam stung my bleeding hands and feet.

Exhaustion crept into my soul. I slept. My mind's eye watched the diminishing torchlights that flickered and faded out of sight on the top of my adventure-filled cliff.

A rainbow-colored mist hovered over a calm turquoise ocean. I felt a warm fur against my cheek. I opened my eyes to discover that I was lying on otter-fur blankets in a small cave. Outside the cave was a sandy beach protected by a high rock cliff

A red smell, like something broiled, attracted my hunger. I followed my nose. I found a basket of warm roasted fish in the back of the cave. Suddenly, something snarled. I paused. A small feisty beast peered its eyes at me through a mask of black hair. Then it resumed chewing on its juicy piece of fish. I laughed. I stomped my foot to scare it away. The critter peeked at me. I hesitated. Then it relaxed and resumed masticating on its fish breakfast.

I felt the loneliness of being ignored. I sensed the shame of being outwitted by a small animal. Desperate, I searched for a rock or a stick to throw at the monster. I found a small semiprecious pebble. *In the hand of David, this would kill Goliath*, I thought. Then, I lobbed it to hit the giant's glistening black nose.

The surprise caused the critter to drop his fish and run out of the cave.

I ran to the basket. With both hands, I held my fish for munching. The juices poured down the sides of my mouth. I reached for another morsel. A terrific tang of trout tickled my tongue. While I was reaching for another morsel, I heard a deep laughter. I turned. Against the bright yellow sunlight at the mouth of the cave, I saw the umber silhouette of a naked man.

Like my masked predecessor, I ran to escape. But a strong hand grabbed my wrist. It pulled me flat against its barren body. I froze. Then I recognized the feeling of that hand. It held the same vibrations as the hand that held me above the rocks and waves last night.

I relaxed. His body warmed me. I sighed. My cheek brushed his chest. My body began to tingle.

Then he pushed me away, saying, "Don't you want to finish your breakfast?"

I recognized Silver Fox. "Thank you for saving me last night."

"I heard that you would be searching for a cave to hide in. So I paddled my canoe to the rocky cliffs nearest to the presidio."

"You found this cave for me."

"Yes. It's an old friend of mine. I use it to relax when I am troubled."

"I guess that I couldn't be more troubled than anybody right now."

"Your friends are safe in the cave on Monte Madonna. You will be safe here."

"But the inquisitor will send troops looking for me."

"This cave is far down the coast from the presidio. The soldiers have never been here. They are afraid of the grizzly bears and the mountain lions."

"Did you bring the fish in the basket?

"Yes. I caught it this morning and cooked it while you slept."

"Thank you. And the masked robber thanks you too."

"Oh. You mean Bandit, my pet raccoon."

"Are all the animals and birds your friends?"

"Oh, we like to live together as friends, but sometimes we question one another's idea of friendship."

"Ha ha! Now, I know we are all God's creatures." My laughter began to warm my thoughts and my body. I beckoned with my outspread hands toward the basket of fish. I looked with my two eyes at Silver Fox. I realized that my eye patch was gone. "Here. Let us partake of this palatial feast that you and your friends the fish have provided for us."

"Welcome to our Calendaruc hospitality."

"I hope to enjoy a long experience of you and your friends' kindness." I reached for my fish meal. Its flavor enkindled my taste buds, and its aroma teased my nostrils. My stomach yearned for more. Silver Fox and I ate and ate. Finally, Bandit reappeared. We all ate together as friends.

Full, I patted my belly. Then I noticed my new clothes, or lack of clothes. Around my waist was a short, short skirt of otter belts, a gift from my otter friends. Around my neck reclined a generous garland of green kelp and small seashells, a gift from the sea and my crustacean friends. I blushed. Then I eyeballed Silver Fox.

"Your clothes must have fallen off on the cliff and in the water last night. I dressed you as best I could. We don't use a lot of clothing, as your people have noticed. Nakedness is natural for us. Don't be afraid. Our laws are very strict about sexual relations before marriage."

"Thank you. I appreciate your frankness. And I want to know more about your people's laws about everything."

"We are forbidden to speak about the dead. We know little about our history as a people. Obedience, moderation, and cooperation with family and tribe members are our way of life. Our way of life has been passed down to us through our elders from one generation to the next. So far, it has been successful for thousands of generations. But now, we see an interruption. The new people, your people, have come with guns and cannons. They take our women as slaves and prostitutes. The soldiers rape our girls and women. Our men and boys are made slaves. Some are deported back to Spain as slaves."

"Yes, I understand. I am a Gypsy. In Spain, we are considered less than human. Spaniards can kill us without any remorse."

"How can you remain with these people who persecute your people?"

"We have no place, no country of our own," I moaned.

"The same thing is happening here as has happened in the country of the Aztecs."

"Yes, Columbus and his followers, like Cortez, claimed all these lands for God and the king of Spain." My hands smoothed the otter fur of my skirt. I thought to myself, *These innocent people do not know what's in for them.*

"Padre Antonio seems like a good person. He tries to protect us from the soldiers. We like him. He teaches us to plant fruit trees and vegetables. We have always found plants in the hills for seeds and fruit to eat. Now we can harvest food closer to our village."

"Yes, he is good. His order is a good part of the church. They are here to help the native people. But the Spanish government is using them. They used the Jesuits at first to convert the native people into real Spaniards. But they were so successful that the unsuccessful Spaniards here made the king and the pope condemn them so that they could seize their flourishing rancheros for themselves."

I watched Silver Fox's face. His eyes remained fixed without emotion. As if he knew what was in store for himself and his people.

"I will have to speak to my elders. They will tell us what to do."

I thought to myself, *These people are so far ahead of us in some ways. Padre Antonio has told us that these people accept same-sex marriages, both males and females, in their villages. Our king and the pope are nowhere near that custom.*

Silver Fox jumped up from our dining room floor. He shook the sand off his haunches. With extended hands, he offered to help me up. I grabbed his hands. He pulled me up. I smiled and studied the tattoos on his face. These marks indicated his family's tribelet and animal image.

I was accustomed to his nakedness. It seemed so natural to me now. I wanted to be the same. But the otter skirt and the seaweed garland were his gifts to me. I had to wear them as an act of appreciation. I really liked them. They were so comfortable after the heavy, bulky Gypsy man's pantaloons and jacket. I was crazy about them. *Wait till Safira sees me in this!* Silver Fox gave his foxiest glance at me. He looked like he did not know what to say. Could he say what he felt, or must he ask his elders for their advice?

"We may be here for a good while." He paused. "Would you like to go for a swim?"

"Bandit looks like he would choose to go for a swim, and so would I. Let's go."

We walked out of our cave into the bright sunlight. The blue-green sea with its white foam waves enticed us to dive into its arms. The high cliffs, on the other hand, beckoned us to stretch our legs and feel the exhilaration of exhausted muscles.

I gazed at Silver Fox. He was taller than me. He was shorter than my brother, Christabo, and Henrique, but his *bicho* was bigger. I challenged, "Last one to the top of the cliff is a rotten apple."

"You're on!" His well-muscled body churned and throbbed like a dinosaur in heat. Sweat flew from his body like rain from a cloudburst.

I followed his trail of perspiration. My fatigue won. I walked the rest of the way.

"Hello, you rotten apple," he laughed.

I collapsed in his arms. He held me for an instant. Then he raised me high above his head.

He stood with me high above him.

"Do you see that swirling ring in the sea? It can pull you down to the bottom of the sea where you can live forever with the sea-god. Many lovers leap from here to there."

"Why would they do that?" I asked.

"For some reason that keeps them from living together in their village." He put me down with my feet on the ground.

I looked at the huge whirlpool. I felt its alluring charm of hope for unfortunate lovers. Who would think that these primitive people could have the emotion similar to that of a Greek god?

For weeks, Silver Fox and I enjoyed each other's company in our private cave with Bandit. Once a week, Silver Fox would take his tule canoe up the coast to learn the news about the inquisitor from his native friends. So far, the news was always the same. He was searching for his heretics.

We held our breath and waited.

CHAPTER 12

Gypsy eyes emoted pain.

Clapping hands held joy.

Hope danced over ragged rocks.

Seagulls flew homeward.

Silver Fox and I lived together for over a month. I wanted to marry him. A Gypsy wedding, with a quick cut on the palms of our left hands to mingle our blood, would make us one. But I knew his native customs would never allow it. They required a meeting of the parents to gain their approval. The gifts from both families to one another must happen before any consent to the marriage could occur.

All that Silver Fox did for me was, in his mind, an act of kindness for a friend.

We enjoyed our friendship. There were meals of many of our other friends: fish, abalones, quail, and otters, to mention a few.

We swam. We hiked. We climbed the cliff. My leg muscles grew stronger. I learned to keep up with his trail of perspiration. But I remained a rotten apple.

"Jaca, I'm going to canoe to my friends to find out what's happening. Stay here with Bandit. Is there anything that you would want me to ask them?"

"Yes. Ask if my friends are safe."

"I should be back by tonight." He waved and shoved off in his tule canoe.

As the sun began to set in a sky of orange and gold, I saw Silver Fox's canoe touch shore.

"What news have you?" I asked.

He replied, "Padre Fernando Salmanez has organized a search party to hunt down you and your people. He won't stop until you're all burned at the stake."

"Oh! I knew that he wouldn't stop. His hatred is so unholy for a padre."

"He is the inquisitor."

"Yes. He'll never give up. What can I do?"

"Your friends are still in the cave on Monte Madonna. Padre Antonio has come down to take care of the Mission Santa Lucia."

"What does Padre Fernando know?"

"He has been told that all of you have left to live with the Russians at Fort Ross."

"That's good!" I sat down on a rock to rest.

"Padre Franco Gonzalez keeps telling the inquisitor that you are all out of his jurisdiction and that he should go back to Spain."

"Has it worked?"

"No. He still insists on searching. He will turn up every stone to find you. His hatred is horrendous for heretics."

I thought to myself, *Maybe I should give myself up. If he could kill me, he might forget about all the others.*

"Silver Fox, when you go to see Padre Antonio, ask him for a mission garment for me. I want to go up to see him, but I must wear mission clothes."

"Why do you want to see him?"

"I have a plan to save my friends."

"The grizzly bear has whispered in your ear. Be careful. He has long sharp teeth."

"You have taught me what it means to be a friend. Now it's my turn to prove my friendship."

Silver Fox looked hard into my eyes. He saw my thoughts. His eyes closed tight. He spoke in a whisper, "Tomorrow we will canoe up to Padre Antonio. I have a mission garment for you and me. I will make a garland of green kelp for your neck."

A bright sunny morning made the trip by canoe easy. We arrived at the mouth of the Rio del Pajaro. Silver Fox paddled upstream until we came to the trail that led to the meadow of the Mission Santa Lucia. There we left the canoe. We walked under the redwood trees until we came to the meadow and our tule huts. The roses of Castile were sprouting where Catalina and Safira had planted them. Padre Antonio and the natives were making adobe bricks.

"Welcome," called Padre Antonio. He stood up from his brick-making and brushed his hands free of adobe dust. "I'm glad to see that you are safe. What can I do for you?"

"I want to know how we can solve our problem with Padre Fernando."

"He has doubled his attempt to search for you. And he is questioning the natives."

"Yes," added Silver Fox. "My father and mother have told that to me too."

"Yesterday, he had a native whipped. But the poor man did not say anything."

"So far my family is safe," sighed Silver Fox. "My little sister, Song Bird, asks the grizzly bear spirit to eat him up."

"I hope that my friends can stay in the cave on Monte Madonna."

"Yes, I send food for them," answered Padre Antonio. "Old Corte asks about you."

"Does he know that I am a woman?"

"He claims that you are his daughter."

"His daughter?" I fumbled for words. "How is that possible?"

"He and Safira say that you are their love child."

"How does Grast feel about that?"

"Well, he accepts that as something that happened before he and Safira married."

"Now, I know that I've got to get them to Russia and safety. Could we get ready to leave today?"

"Yes," responded Padre Antonio. "We could climb to their cave and go over the hill to the next valley and head inland to Fort Ross."

"That sounds good to me." I smiled at Silver Fox, and I wondered, *Would he come with us or stay with his people?*

Then a runner, all out of breath, came into the mission area. He stopped and fell to his knees before Padre Antonio.

"Welcome, Blue Possum. What is your news?" asked Padre Antonio.

"I have bad news. Please forgive me, Padre." He looked at Silver Fox and began to cry. "The padre from the presidio has taken Song Bird to be whipped until she tells where the heretics are."

I grabbed Silver Fox and hugged him. He remained calm. I knew that he was thinking. I waited. *What would he do?*

"We must go to the presidio," declared Padre Antonio.

"Yes," declared Silver Fox. "We must save my sister."

Padre Antonio sent some natives to tell the people in the cave on Monte Madonna what had happened. Then he prepared to go with us to the presidio.

We arrived at the presidio after a three-hour walk. Outside the front gate, we found Silver Fox's mother and father and tribe members. Silver Fox comforted his parents.

Then the gate opened. Padre Fernando Salmanez stood before us. He glared at us and said, "The girl refuses to tell us where the heretics are."

I raised my arms and hands high. "Here I am. Take me! Let the child go!"

Padre Fernando smiled. He could not believe his ears and eyes. "Seize that heretic!"

I did not struggle as the soldiers grabbed me and bound me with their ropes and chains. They dragged me inside the gate. There, on the ground, I saw the bloody back of the dead girl, Song Bird. I cried, "You monster! How dare you call yourself a padre!"

The soldiers threw Song Bird's body outside the gate to land at the feet of her parents. Then they slammed the gate shut.

I heard the wailing and sobbing of Silver Fox's people. I wept.

"Step into my torture chamber," grimaced Padre Fernando Salmanez.

The soldiers led me into the courtyard of the presidio. There waiting for me was the stake. The wooden fagots were already stacked around the stake to burn its next victim—me. The soldiers tied me to the stake. I asked for a cross. One of the soldiers crossed and tied two branches from one of the fagot bundles and handed it to me. "Thank you," I said.

Then two soldiers started to light the fagots. My back felt a slight jarring movement in the stake. Then it came again. This time it was harder. The flames grew higher and hotter.

The soldiers cried out, "Earthquake!" They began to run every which way. The earth began to open cracks across the courtyard. The main gate of the presidio cracked open, and Silver Fox and his tribe members, along with my friends from the cave, flew into the courtyard.

The flames encircled me. I cried my last prayer as loud as I could, "Jesus, have mercy on me, a sinner."

Through the flames, I saw Grast and my father, Corte, trying to scatter the flaming fagots. But their efforts were in vain. I died. The pain from the flames was short-lived. At first, I felt a numbness. Then I became a part of a bright light that had no beginning or an end to its wonder. I could see the courtyard. I looked down on it. There in one of the cracks that had opened and closed during the earthquake lay the stunned body of Padre Fernando. The lower part of his body was caught in the closed crevice. He held out his hands, begging for help. Fra Pablo, who I recognized as my brother, Christabo, was trying to pull him out of the crevice. Padre Antonio and Padre Franco tried to help. But the earth held him too tightly for them to move him. Grast and Corte, unable to save me from the flames, turned and saw the padre in need. Being generous men, they came to help the padres help their companion. The earth moved again. A little after-rumble shook and opened the ground around the padre. With one quick pull, the five pulled the victim to safety. Padre Fernando Salmanez thanked the five for helping him. He recognized the two heretics who helped and thanked them again. Then he called for his donkey. "I must get out of California and its earthquakes today."

Silver Fox began to gather my ashes into a bag. He walked up the Rio Pajaro to where we had left his canoe. He paddled down the river to the ocean and down to our private cave. There, he took my ashes up to the top of our cliff and jumped down into the whirlpool, a swirling ring of the sea that would unite us together with his sea-god forever.

My mind's eye caught Padre Fernando on his donkey on his way back to Spain. I know that God will give him the grace to repent. But will he have the faith to use it?

The End

CPSIA information can be obtained at www.ICGtesting.com
Printed in the USA
LVIW01n1156170815
450418LV00007B/20